An Act of Murder

An Act of Murder

A Professor Prather Mystery

MARY ANGELA

CAMEL PRESS

Seattle, WA

PRESS

Camel Press
PO Box 70515
Seattle, WA 98127

For more information go to: www.camelpress.com
www.maryangelabooks.com

Cover design by Sabrina Sun

An Act of Murder
Copyright © 2016 by Mary Angela

ISBN: 978-1-60381-375-4 (Trade Paper)
ISBN: 978-1-60381-376-1 (eBook)

Library of Congress Control Number: 2016943760

Printed in the United States of America

Acknowledgments

—

MY DAD PASSED away just a few weeks before Camel Press accepted this novel for publication. Had he been with us, he would have been overjoyed at the news. He was a longtime supporter of my writing—and everything else. I am eternally grateful for his unconditional love and dedicate this book to him.

As I wrote and revised this novel, my mom gave me more help and advice than any daughter has a right to expect. Thank you, Mom, for your unwavering support. Your belief in me makes anything possible.

My husband, too, encouraged me at every turn of this adventure, which wasn't always an adventure but often a dark and dubious path. Thank you, Quintin, for giving me a strong shoulder to lean on.

Every day, my daughters remind me what an extraordinary gift life truly is. To see them find delight in my work is an unexpected treasure. Thank you, Madeline and Maisie. You are my greatest blessings.

Finally, thank you to Camel Press and their editorial team, especially Catherine, Jennifer, and Rebecca. Your ideas, suggestions, and revisions amounted to the best writing class I never took.

Prologue

—

DEATH TEACHES US humility. This is what I thought as I walked into the single-road graveyard, becoming more aware with each step the life it took to walk and talk and breathe. It was no easy task, to stay alive, and yet the majority of us managed to do so, and often into old age. But here was an exception, *a tragedy*, and I wondered at its meaning while I traversed the uneven ground. As an English professor, I would have told my students that tragedies were meant to teach us as much about good as evil. I tried to apply that philosophy now and failed.

The good was in life, the walking down this brown path surrounded by sturdy trees. I couldn't help but feel this way as my boots crunched the dead leaves that littered the dirt lane. Had he been alive, my student would have enjoyed this walk. He would have found beauty in its peace and remoteness. I smiled. He might even have found poetry.

The gravestone was small and freshly placed, and as I stood at the marker, a terrific wind came up in the trees. The branches swayed to and fro, making me dizzy with the sheer force of their movement. The wind continued to bend through the branches and bushes until it found me, reassuring like a childhood prayer. I knelt down, my slim book of verse in hand, and read the poem he had chosen for my class. It had always been one of my favorites.

Chapter One

———

IT WAS FALL at the university, and the campus teemed with life—booksellers stocking tightly bound textbooks, professors copying last-minute syllabi, and freshmen hustling into the dorms with cheaply purchased furniture. The chokecherries and honeysuckle flourished, too, and soon I would watch the orange and red leaves fall from the maple trees to the trampled grass of this little-known Midwestern campus. With the opening of a window, gone were the laws of Newton and *Poetics* of Aristotle. Replacing them were the sights and sounds of earthy prairie life, never far beyond the classroom in this small college town.

Copper Bluff, situated in the eastern corner of South Dakota, gave way to a river and lush bottomland. Most of the town was surrounded by fields of soybean, alfalfa, and corn, though the neighboring state had the monopoly on corn. Or so I'd been told. With more moderate weather, they had nothing to do but spread the seeds and watch them grow, an old farmer once said. He didn't have to convince me. I couldn't get anything to grow in my garden except a rhubarb plant, which I had nothing to do with. Yet I never grew tired of trying, and this perseverance was as much a part of this place as anything else. Its spirit, its *sine qua non*.

My house was surrounded by shade, and although I knew little about growing things, I imagined sunshine was rather important to sustainable growth. The trees on Oxford Street were so large that only stray rays of sunlight penetrated the leafy foliage that formed a makeshift canopy over the road. Hostas grew copiously around the front rail of my porch, relishing the shade of the towering pine trees dividing my lot from my neighbor's. A nice-sized bungalow, my house was a block from the campus and a beautiful shade of yellow. I took pride in the fact that I was able to purchase a house and didn't have to rent one of the split-up places at the end of the block. I had lived in plenty of those as a student. Still, my 1917 home had required a good deal of hard work when I moved in a year ago. I had pruned bushes, painted rooms, and torn out carpet, all before giving my first lecture, but it was worth it. The location allowed me to walk to and from campus, a necessity since my only mode of transportation was a red '69 Mustang convertible, a car I'd bought cheap from an uncle who owned a body shop. When my dad scoffed at its impracticality, his brother simply responded with, "She hails from Detroit. Her car oughta have character." My dad relented more easily than I thought he would, probably because the car was inexpensive, but I still hoped to restore it when time and money permitted.

Tonight my meatballs balanced precariously in a Crock Pot on the bucket seat beside me. I was headed for the biannual potluck, and the entire English department was convening at the chair's house for good beginning-of-the-year karma. Although I didn't go out of my way to avoid these events—as did Ralph Carmichael, our British scholar who had famously declined the last fifteen years because of a feud over his office hours—I didn't look forward to them either. We were an awkward bunch, better at reading than conversing, and I'm certain most of us would have been delighted to quit the gatherings altogether. The Christmas party was even more problematic, for it included alcohol and a band, and the creative writers invariably got drunk and started reciting eighteenth-century poetry, or worse, their own. I myself was not immune to the festivities and did no small amount of damage to my own reputation the previous year when I joined in with my rendition of the Stones' "Nineteenth Nervous Breakdown."

This year, though, I'd sworn to avoid volatile discussions with my good friend Lenny Jenkins, our early American literature scholar, always a bad influence on me. He and I inevitably landed on the transcendentalists, and our conversation would become spirited with themes such as *nonconformity*. Our conversation last year had inspired my solo performance, and he'd gladly joined in at every refrain. I rolled my eyes at the very thought of it. Well, there would be no music tonight—and no red wine. I had sworn off it for good measure. I would attend the party, serve my meatballs, thank the chair, and leave.

Jim Giles was a smart man and a decent chair, and I admired the fact that he effectively ignored almost every crisis that occurred in the English department with satisfactory results. Already several cars were parked at his house, a blue Queen Anne much admired throughout the town. His wife, Katherine, was an excellent decorator and hostess who always made even the teaching assistants feel welcome. No matter what one brought, she always exclaimed, "That's just what I was looking for! Put it near the fruit salad, won't you?"

I adjusted the belt to my dark jeans and buttoned the single button on my brown jacket. I preferred my orange jacket because I favored bold colors, but the night air was muggy, so I'd stayed with the brown one, which was both lightweight and professional. As one of the younger faculty members at twenty-eight years old, I was always searching for ways to look *professional*. My hair—curly and resistant to all products with the words "smoothing" in them—did little to aid in my search. Tonight, most of it stayed put in an informal twist, except for several chestnut brown curls that had sprung loose from their pins while I hurried around the kitchen making my dish for the potluck.

The Crock Pot was heavy, and luckily Katherine met me at the door before I could attempt to ring the bell.

"It's so good to see you, Emmeline. Come in, come in," said Katherine.

"Hi, Kate, how are you?" I said.

She led me to the dining room, where a buffet was arranged. Several platters adorned the table, a cheese fondue displayed in the middle.

"Good, good. Glad fall is here. I'm so tired of this humidity, aren't you? Oh, your meatballs! Let's see. I don't have a plug-in that'll reach that far. Let's just put them … here," she said, placing them on a remote sideboard. "There now. Would you like a drink?"

"Just water, thank you."

"Em Prather, I hope you haven't sworn off alcohol tonight on my account."

It was Lenny. His was a friendly young face, with wicked blue eyes, an amazing dimple, and hair that rivaled a boy-band rock star's. It was thick and blond-streaked and stuck up nicely on the top of his head. Perhaps it was our similar ages or perhaps it was our passionate talks that made us such good friends. It certainly wasn't our scholarly pursuits; he studied American literature, and I studied French. Whatever it was, it had brought me closer to him than any of the other five thousand people on campus. I tried to ignore this fact, since I was determined to focus on the important aspects of my career, such as publications and tenure. But I often wondered, if not for his haphazard dating record and my fear of losing his friendship, whether he and I could have been more than friends.

He opened the Crock Pot next to mine and stirred its contents with a large wooden spoon.

"Hey, Lenny, what did you bring?" I asked, looking over his shoulder.

"Beanies and weenies." More quietly, he added, "You know nobody brings a goddamn thing of substance to these things. I'm tired of walking away hungry. Good. You brought meatballs. Ha!"

"One glass of water with a twist of lemon," said Kate, handing me a pretty amber tumbler. "Go sit. Go sit." She motioned in the direction of the living room before flittering away.

"They've sworn off plastic bottles. The *environment*," said Lenny.

I shuffled toward the front room, still puzzling over the placement of my meatballs. Were they comparable to Lenny's mystery bean dish? I remembered Kate complimenting me on them last fall—or perhaps commenting on them. Now that I thought about it, I didn't remember exactly what she had said.

Lenny fell into the one comfortable armchair in the corner, leaving me to scan the room for an appropriate place to sit. I decided on the settee, small and antique and right next to Lenny. The only other option was a folding chair beside Jane Lemort, a woman I avoided whenever possible. There was no subject she didn't profess to have studied in some way, shape, or form.

"How was your summer?" Lenny continued. "I just got back from Massachusetts myself. I saw Walden Pond … visited Emerson's grave. I told him about you. He said you missed your calling."

I perched carefully on the edge of the settee, remembering now how easy it was to become ensnared in Lenny's conversations. "And whatever would that be? Rock star extraordinaire?"

"Just add Merlot," he said, "and *voilà*! She goes from linguist to soloist."

I chuckled. "I would consider the performance more of a duet."

"If that makes you feel better. But you were definitely singing louder than I was." He took a drink from his glass, probably full of bourbon. "Hey, have you met Thomas—what's his last name—Cook? Is he going to be here tonight?"

"No, but I want to. I heard he wrote his entire dissertation over the rhetoric on cereal boxes."

"You're kidding," he said, placing his drink on the hardwood floor.

I tossed him a cloth coaster from the nearby end table. "I'm not. I read it somewhere … or maybe somebody told me."

"Yeah, books and people are the same."

"You don't believe me."

Now he showed his dimple. "Of course I believe you, Em. It's just that more than once you've told me things that I've believed to be the gospel, even repeated them, and then came to find out you've read them in some novel."

"Well you know how it is. Reading for the *Copper Bluff Review*, the upcoming edition of *Modern French Studies*, students' essays—a novel here and there for enjoyment. It's easily done … to remember a thing and not really know where it came from."

"You told me Jimmy Hoffa was found," he shot back.

"That. Well," I crossed my ankles, admiring my chocolate suede high heels, "that was part of a *very* intriguing series. Honestly, some nights I didn't know if I'd been dreaming or reading or watching the news. It was all-encompassing." I sighed. "And he was *almost* found. I mean, they thought they found his body once. I don't know. I remember it being somewhere north of Detroit."

"Please, please—help yourselves to the food. There is a wonderful assortment. Just everything," said Kate, swooping in and out of the rooms like a ballroom dancer.

I stood up.

"Saved by the hostess," said Lenny, following behind me.

"I'll ask him. Just wait. If we see him tonight, I'll ask him," I said.

"Jimmy Hoffa?"

I turned to glare at him over my shoulder. "Clever, Lenny. I meant Thomas Cook."

There were at least twenty-five people, most of them in line, and it seemed we came in last. I didn't mind, though. I was in no hurry to try Lenny's beans and weenies, and I knew he would insist.

"Lenny, welcome back. Emmeline, how are you?" asked Jim Giles, the chair of the English department. He wore a traditional corduroy jacket, with velvet elbow patches and tan pants. In his hand he carried a very large cup of coffee. To me, he looked like a person who belonged in front of a typewriter, surrounded by newspaper men and cigarettes.

"Hello, Jim. It's good to be back," I said.

"You say that now. Just wait until Monday," said Giles.

"It's not Monday I'm worried about. It's October," said Lenny.

We laughed and kept moving. A toffee-colored tablecloth covered the modern kitchen island, along with Depression dinnerware and petite vases of black-eyed Susans. I took a dainty glass plate and moved toward the archway that separated the kitchen and dining room. Several dishes filled the formal table, and I sampled everything that was left, making sure to leave room for my meatballs. Lenny was pondering the cheese fondue, so now was my chance to approach the sideboard. I opened the lid and frowned, spooning out three meatballs from the stack.

"Hey, leave some for me," said Lenny, standing behind me.

"Don't worry. There are plenty left," I mumbled, giving him the spoon.

"Jackpot," he said. "You have to try mine. It's not just beans and hotdogs. I have a spice in there."

"Ah. A secret ingredient. Sorry. No room." I shrugged.

The front parlor was full; even the settee was taken. I found an empty chair in the living room adjoining the kitchen. The space was still rather formal yet had a small stereo and speakers from which, I imagined, NPR crackled on Saturday mornings. I imagined a lot of things about a lot of people. No more than an eighth of it was probably true. For all I knew, Giles rocked out in full stereo surround sound and had a fifty-inch plasma tucked safely downstairs. People were astonishing when you got to know them.

The fondue was good and so was the tofu, really, although it wasn't as much fun eating it without Lenny around. Last year's teaching assistants were amusing, though, as they recounted their worst teaching moments—there seemed to be many and sundry—to the new teaching assistants.

A man entered with a delicate looking woman at his side. They were a good-looking couple, maybe from the East Coast, their clothing a blend of grays and blacks. The couple's plates were nearly empty, and I wondered if they had been mingling and eating or hadn't eaten yet at all. They scanned the room for a place to sit, and as if eager to please, two teaching assistants stood up and walked toward the kitchen.

"Hello," I said, sticking out my hand. "I don't believe we've met. I'm Emmeline Prather."

"Emma-leen or Emma-line?" the man said.

"Emmeline, like Caroline. French but from Detroit."

"Got it," he said.

"Hi," said the woman.

They began to converse intimately, and I sat looking on as if watching a foreign-language film. "Are you new to the department?" I broke in.

"Oh, yes. I'm sorry. I'm Thomas Cook, and this is my wife, Lydia."

"Thomas Cook!" I exclaimed, looking around for Lenny, who was nowhere in sight.

Thomas looked sort of shocked, and I immediately apologized. "It's just that my friend and I were discussing your dissertation before dinner. You wrote it about cereal boxes, correct?"

His wife smiled patiently.

"Well, I guess you could say that." Now he smiled back at his wife.

"What *would* you say? I mean, what would be an accurate representation of your thesis?" I asked.

He handed his wife his plate as if he were about to stand and give a soliloquy. "In short, it examines the consequences of health rhetoric, more specifically organic rhetoric, on health-conscious consumers."

I slowly chewed and swallowed my meatball as I thought of how to respond. "You must have eaten quite a few boxes of cereal."

"It was seven hundred and fifty pages by the time it was finished, and I had barely unearthed the deep tomb of a very new field of study," he said.

"He was accepted by seven different PhD schools," his wife added.

I said nothing. I was still evaluating his metaphor.

"But that was just luck," he said. "Organic was novel at the time."

I nodded. "I'd never get by with writing a dissertation on the French Romantics today."

"Yes, well, death of the author and all that," he laughed.

"No one will talk me into killing off my authors. French or not, Foucault—"

"Please tell me I did not just hear Em use the 'F' word," said Judd Turner, who taught literary criticism. "I'm going to save you right now, Thomas, and tell Em that Kate is serving red velvet cake in the dining room."

"I was just … red velvet? I thought she saved that for Christmas," I said.

"She told me to tell you especially," Judd said.

"It *is* my favorite," I said to Thomas and Lydia. "You must try it. It simply melts in your mouth."

"Lydia cannot digest gluten," said Thomas.

"Well, it was good to meet you anyway. I mean, it was good to meet you. Not despite the gluten." I stuck out my hand, and Thomas shook it briskly. "I'm sure I'll see you on campus."

"Yes, of course," he said. "I look forward to it." Lydia simply leaned into him.

Kate served me an especially large helping of cake, and I balanced it carefully as I went in search of Lenny. He had somehow found his corner armchair and was in the middle of a heated exchange with Jane Lemort, our medievalist. The only clue that gave away his irritation was his bright red ear tips, which he probably could have blamed on the drink. Despite the fact that I wanted to tell him about Thomas Cook, I was about to walk away when he caught my eye and silently pleaded with me to join their conversation.

"Em! How's the cake?"

I rested my hands on the back of a nearby folding chair. I did not want to commit to sitting down. "Excellent, as always. Hi, Jane. Lenny, Thomas Cook *is* here and he *did* write his dissertation on cereal boxes."

"No shit," said Lenny.

I smiled widely. "He's right back there if you want to visit with him."

"What did you say?" asked Lenny.

"I just asked him about his dissertation, and he told me. It's seven hundred and fifty pages."

Lenny whistled.

"Does that surprise you, Lenny? I would think quite a few dissertations reach that length," said Jane, sounding very much like a psychologist.

"Yeah, the ones on *War and Peace*," said Lenny, laughing.

"Popular culture may be the *War and Peace* of our time," said Jane.

"Are cereal boxes considered pop culture now? Christ," said Lenny.

"I'll tell you what pop culture is. Pop culture is a poor excuse to write about a bunch of bird brains running around a desolate island planning each other's demises, all for a chance at fifteen minutes on *Good Morning America*," I said. This addition to the conversation came out just as silence fell over the room, making it seem louder and more brazen than intended. Equally unnerving was the fact that Thomas Cook stood in the doorway of the dining room, freezing momentarily before pouring his coffee, which sat next to the cake.

Jane stood and left, making her excuses first, and people began to converse in normal tones again.

Lenny finished his glass of bourbon in one gulp. Now he was the one smiling. "I assume, by the look on your face, that that man over there grinding his teeth is our Thomas Cook?"

AFTER THE POTLUCK, I retreated to my small office on campus in Harriman Hall. It was connected to a larger office belonging to Jim Giles, and I often wondered if the space was truly his storage closet. But this was of little consequence to me. The location provided me with ample opportunity to overhear situations much graver than mine—Ed Ludvar's evaluations, Jen Hoyka's third mental breakdown, Judd Turner's affairs with his freshmen. And although the room always smelled of pine cleaner and textbooks, in the late-day haze hung the very essence of a September evening. A small, battered desk and two side-by-side bookshelves occupied the longest wall in the room, while the corner alcove boasted a long, rectangular window with a mismatched chair and ottoman.

Because I had trouble sleeping, I often took late-night walks around the campus, enamored by its thoughtful stillness. I would also come to sit and watch out this window. Tonight, the fireflies danced near the water fountain in the courtyard. As fall progressed, the leaves would form makeshift ground blizzards. In the winter, nothing would happen at all, save the snowflakes piling atop the garden wall like tiny building blocks. Then spring would arrive like a benediction, falling from the blithe note of a robin, and the school year would end as pleasantly as it had started.

Of course there would be the in-between, but that was rather interesting, too. The straight-A student, the apathetic football player, the quiet genius ... I looked forward to meeting them all again. They had their own stories to tell in their required semester of composition. Although my PhD was in French literature, I taught English because the campus had no genuine French Department. It was a compromise, and one that wasn't entirely unexpected. More diverse campuses could be found in larger cities, but growing up in Detroit, I longed for a different lifestyle. My dad blamed it on my name, which belonged to my great-great grandmother; he said it put romantic ideas in my head.

Yet there *was* something romantic—nostalgic, even—about Copper Bluff's unending flatness, its immutability. There were no abandoned factories, no slum neighborhoods. Only the wind ravaged the buildings; only the snow felt cold. I fell in love with it when I did my graduate work at the University of Chicago and submitted a paper on redefining women's work in the pioneer novel for a conference at Copper Bluff. My parents, shocked at the idea of my remaining in the Midwest, promised to make me repay my tuition if I didn't take my expensive education East, and I didn't blame them. They had saved every penny they ever made so that I could go to my dream universities and better my future. The problem was I had been raised with a sensibility I could not reconcile with the Ivy League schools. I too often found myself on the side of the have-nots to throw my lot in with the haves. I took the open assistant professor position in Copper Bluff the day after I took my oral exams and had been repaying my parents ever since.

I stood and peered out my office window, across the courtyard. Even now, a year later, I wouldn't alter my decision if I could. Besides the picturesque town and the tranquil campus, there was André Duman and the prospect of a French Department.

André Duman had been hired several years ago when the Spanish teacher went on sabbatical, and there was a need for a part-time Romance language instructor. Although his original assignment had been temporary, the university kept him on as an adjunct. Soon he became determined to begin a French Department and set up a resource room for French language students and a movie night that was always well attended by females of various pursuits. When his department got going, he promised, there would be a need for a French literature teacher—which was my specialty—and I hung on to his promise as if it were a grape at the end of the harvest, the sweetness of it growing with each day.

I sat down, hoping to finish my novel, a gothic romance, before the semester officially began tomorrow. I just couldn't. My mind wandered from the novel to André to the potluck, and I read several more pages before realizing I could remember nothing. I shut the book for good. Instead, I turned on my computer and logged on to my campus account. I printed all three of my class rosters, scanning the lists for students I knew or names I recognized. In all, there were sixty-one students, sixty-one people I would come to know quite well over the course of the next sixteen weeks. After years as a teaching assistant and professor, the idea was still thrilling.

I tucked the rosters safely away in their respective folders and the folders into my worn leather satchel. Then I turned off the light and locked the door behind me.

The English Department was on the second floor of Harriman Hall, and the narrow stairwell always smelled of paint. This I attributed to the constant detection of asbestos and the maintenance crew's commitment to covering it up. Thus, the blast of air I received when I opened the back door was welcoming. On most occasions, I used the front entrance, which connected Harriman Hall to the rest of the campus. But because I had driven straight from the potluck, I'd used the rear entrance adjacent to the parking lot.

The campus was relatively quiet except for an occasional holler from one of the nearby frat houses and a steady bass beat coming from a parked car somewhere in the vicinity. Very few vehicles occupied the parking lot now, and the *click-click-click* of my heels reverberated among the surrounding buildings as I walked toward my car.

I tugged on the door, only to discover that it was locked, a rarity, and rummaged through my jacket pockets for the keys. My satchel came off my shoulder and the keys fell to the ground with a clang. I knelt down and was fumbling for them in the dark when I overheard voices. Abruptly, I froze. I was in an awkward position; it appeared that I had knelt down beside the car to eavesdrop. I couldn't stand up now. Instead, I studied my shoe and pretended to tie it, despite the fact that it was a high heel with no laces.

I could not see the individuals—they were on the other side of the car—but the voices were male and female, and the two seemed to be quarrelling. Her voice was quiet but insistent. His was easier to hear only because it was deeper.

"I don't want to wait. Why can't you tell him now?" he asked.

They had to be students—impetuous souls. I felt somewhat relieved knowing that if I were detected, it would not be by seasoned faculty members. I had done enough tonight to create a burgeoning divide between my new colleague and me.

"I said I can't," she insisted. "He's not ready."

He was agitated; I could tell by the pacing of his footsteps. "You promised you'd tell him before classes start."

Was I overhearing a lover's spat? If so, it was a bit scant on the love. I detected nothing but bitterness between these two individuals.

"Look," he said, "if you're not going to tell him, I will."

This declaration was met with absolute silence, and I didn't dare take a breath.

"No, you won't," she finally said, growling out each word.

"Oh yeah? And who's going to stop me? You?" He laughed, but I could tell he was nervous.

"Yeah, me. I could make your life a living hell, and you know it."

I was so shaken by the turn of the conversation, I fumbled my keys, and the pair became quiet. I debated whether or not to stand up and confront them. My teacherly instinct said something was amiss, but I worried my actions would be unwelcome—especially for the boy. I knew how sensitive male students at this age could be about their egos.

"Come on," she said, her voice turning softer, "let's go."

"No," he said. "Forget it."

First I heard heavy footsteps leave the parking lot, growing softer, then silent as they reached the grass. Moments later, lighter footsteps started off in another direction.

A sick feeling settled in the bottom of my stomach as I quietly unlocked my car. I slid into the seat and shut the door. What had just happened? I replayed the brief conversation in my head several times, each version growing more sinister. I surveyed the parking lot, but there was no one in sight. I turned the key, and the engine rumbled to a start. I quickly drove the one block to my house, the sick feeling never leaving my stomach.

Chapter Two

———

THE NEXT MORNING was sunny and hot, a reminder that the mild weather of the past few days was not to be expected. The Great Plains was a land of extremes and scorned anything remotely *seasonal.*

A warm west wind filled my ears as I bicycled across campus, avoiding clumps of students standing and talking and laughing. Some students were moving hesitantly, heads down, studying their first-day schedules printed off on flimsy copy paper. One student, a blonde girl, accidentally let hers loose into the wind, and it skipped wildly in my direction. I sped up and swerved off the walkway and onto the grass, nearly trapping it with my tire. Instead the paper flipped up directly in front of my face, and I stupidly let go of the handlebars to catch it. Catch it I did, but not before I lost control of my bike, nearly missing a tree before falling to the ground.

A nearby group of students clapped, and I brushed myself off, readjusted my backpack, and bowed. The pale blonde shuffled up to me, clearly embarrassed, despite the fact that I was the one who had fallen.

I thrust the schedule into her hand and tugged at my sticky shirt. "Here you go. Keep a hold of it."

"Thanks," she mumbled, her eyes never leaving the piece of paper.

I picked up my bike, happy to see there was no damage, and continued toward Harriman Hall.

The smell of coffee filled the air, and I walked down to the faculty lounge to pour myself a cup before heading to my office. The lounge was empty, and the coffee pot nearly was, too, so I could fill up my *Gone with the Wind* movie mug only to the words "Frankly, my dear, I don't give a damn." Then I shut off the pot.

"A quarter a cup, Emmeline," scolded Barb, the department secretary. "I didn't see you put in your quarter."

She had her hands on her large hips, as if making a joke, but I knew how seriously she took the coffee fund.

"I hardly have a quarter's worth here," I said, showing her my half-empty cup.

"I suppose I'll let you go this time," she said. "Just remember to put in two quarters next time."

I scooted past her, attempting a weak smile. "Of course."

"And whoever takes the last cup has to make a fresh pot. Tsk tsk. Have you forgotten everything over the summer?" she added before I was completely out of earshot. I doubled my pace. I felt like a criminal every time I went for the pot. Everybody did. And everybody had talked to Giles about it. His only reply was, "She's just doing her job. Can't blame her for that." It was easy for him to say; Barb had a terrible crush on him and made him coffee, tea, photocopies—favors the rest of us did without. And now she was talking about buying a water cooler, a purchase Giles wholeheartedly agreed would save on plastic bottles. The thought of her rationing Dixie cups was just too much.

In my office, I scanned the bookshelves for my textbooks, small necessities I had forgotten last night. Over the summer,

I had come in to organize my books, tired of seeing them lying about on the table. Of course, I had more books than bookshelves, and several had to be double-stacked. As the minutes until class grew shorter, so did my patience, and soon my thoughtful scanning turned to panicked pillaging.

"Emmeline, what are you looking for over there?"

It was Jim Giles, the chair of our department. The close proximity of our offices had made us good friends despite our age difference.

"My textbooks," I hollered back. I remembered that I had stacked them in my desk hutch so as to keep them close at hand for the upcoming semester. I opened the glass door, which didn't need much encouragement, and out poured writing paper, stamps, and chewing gum. Left in the hutch, however, were three badly worn texts. "Ha!" I said.

Giles chuckled from the doorway. "I take it you found what you were looking for."

Nonchalantly, I scooted the gum under the desk with my shoe as I pulled out the books. "Yes. Here they are."

He viewed me quizzically. "Did you have a … scuffle already this morning?"

Instinctively, I smoothed my hair. It was prone to theatrics the moment I left the house. "No. Why do you say that?"

He pointed to my pants.

"Good god!" I exclaimed, wiping at the grass stain on my tan trousers. It was hard enough to find pants that fit my petite frame, and these were new. I took off my backpack and began searching for the stain remover in the front pocket. "I was riding my bike on campus this morning, and I don't have to tell you what the wind is like today. Anyway, a girl—probably a freshman by the looks of her, pale and ready to cry, you know the type—lost her schedule." I began rubbing the stain remover vigorously across the stain. "There it was, flying across the campus, and she frozen in her tracks. Well, I knew she would rather die than tear after it herself, so what could I do? I chased it down with my bike and returned it to the poor girl."

"And your pants?" he asked.

"Oh right," I said. "I took a small tumble in the process."

"Don't worry," he said. "No one will ever guess."

I looked down to see that the stain remover had soaked a third of my pant leg.

"The wind might not be such a bad thing today after all. It might dry that spot just in time," he said, smiling, as he returned to his office.

I shoved the books in my bag and hurriedly locked up.

The campus courtyard was the one open square not overpopulated with trees, clearing a path for the most beloved building on the grounds: Stanton Hall. Its beautiful Sioux Quartzite looked almost pink against the brilliant blue sky, the white peaks piercing the cloudless air. The building, three stories tall and over a hundred years old, once housed all the classrooms and offices on campus. Today, it still contained several classrooms, a lovely lecture hall, and the Foreign Languages Department.

I made my way up the wide wooden staircase and turned the corner to room 205. All twenty-three students were in attendance, staring at me in complete silence until I opened my bag and smiled. Then their eyes immediately fell to their desks as I retrieved my copies. I passed out the neatly stapled syllabi and began going over class expectations line by line.

"And that concludes the syllabus for Composition 101. You can see our Monday, Wednesday, Friday schedule is attached, so do not lose it. Keeping up with the schedule is paramount to your success in this course." I flipped the final page of the syllabus.

"What if we do lose it?" said a well-dressed boy in the back row. His outfit probably cost more than my mortgage payment.

"Don't," I said. "Any other questions?" I waited several moments. "Let's continue then."

After class, a student came up to me as I was wiping off the chalkboard.

"Professor Prather?"

"Yes?" I said, turning around. The boy had a sand-colored crew cut, a deep tan, and small blue eyes that crinkled as he spoke. The long, muscular arms that stuck out of his checked shirt, however, belied his young face. He looked as though he worked outdoors.

"It says on the syllabus that we have to recite a poem for the literary analysis unit. Does that mean in front of the class?"

I assumed he was talking about page three of the schedule, but his own copy was rolled into a makeshift spyglass, which caused me no small amount of irritation. Still, I remained encouraging. "Yes, but it can be any poem you wish. It doesn't have to be, say, Shakespeare. And it's not due for a couple of weeks. We'll have read lots of poems by then," I assured him.

He acted unperturbed, shoving the syllabus into the mesh pocket of his backpack, but I got the feeling he was carefully choosing his words.

"Do all 101 classes make you do that?" he asked. "Recite poetry?"

"Mine do," I said, smiling pleasantly. "You could try another class, I suppose, if you're really concerned about it. But you can't graduate without taking a semester of composition."

"It's just that I hate poetry," he admitted hesitantly.

"Is that all?" I said. Two thirds of the freshmen I knew hated poetry. It was nothing to drop a class over. "I'll make you a deal. You'll find one poem that you like in this unit, or I'll dig until I find you one you do."

His shoulders relaxed a bit, and a small grin touched the corners of his lips. "I've never read a poem I liked yet."

"Trust me," I said. "I know the right places to look. What are you into? Sports? Music? Girls?"

He was intrigued. I could tell because the grin spread to the rest of his face. But I could also tell he wasn't used to interacting this way with his teachers. He was newly graduated from high school and accustomed to following orders.

"Or perhaps dirt bikes? Dirt roads? *Landscape.* Ooh … maybe Robert Frost."

Now he smiled. I would take it.

"I'll recite the poem. You don't have to go to any trouble."

I could see that he didn't want to make trouble; he wanted to fit in even if that meant reciting poetry. "It's no trouble at all. It's a promise—one I intend to keep."

He slung his backpack over his shoulder and turned to leave. Back at the chalkboard, I erased my name, "Emmeline Prather."

"I saw you, you know."

"Hmm?" I said, turning around.

He was studying me from the doorway, his head cocked to one side. The grin was gone, and the tentativeness was back.

"Oh, this morning, you mean?" I asked vaguely. My mind was already on my next class. "I know. I'm an absolute klutz."

He shook his head, but his grin returned. My self-depreciation seemed to put him at ease. "Forget it. See you Wednesday, Professor."

Forget it. Those were the same words the student in the parking lot had used last evening. Could *this* be the boy from the parking lot, the one who'd kept me tossing and turning all night? Was that where he had seen me? Did he wonder if I had seen him too?

"Wait … what's your name again?" I sputtered.

"Austin Oliver," he called over his shoulder.

"See you Wednesday, Austin Oliver," I said to an empty doorway.

I finished erasing the board then gathered my books and extra syllabi. The room was still now, so it was easy to exaggerate the beauty of it: the long rectangular windows, the hazy sunshine streaming over several wooden desks, the dust particles settling upon the ancient podium. Although Stanton Hall was the oldest building on campus, it had been remodeled several years ago with the convenience of air conditioning, a luxury that was afforded fewer than half of the buildings on campus. Indeed, all my other classes were in buildings like Harriman Hall, which barely provided heating for the long months of the winter, let alone central cooling for the short months of summer.

There was one more reason I enjoyed the building so much, I thought, as I walked down the open staircase to the second floor: André Duman. There he was, placed among the German and Spanish and Lakota teachers, who were much more in demand and better funded. The window to the Foreign Languages Department was small and beveled, and I nearly had to stand flush with the door to see in. There in the corner, his small desk directly behind the secretary's, sat André, typing furiously at his laptop while stopping frequently to think and gesticulate with his hands. Once in a while, a dark lock escaped from his mop of hair and jerked to and fro to the beat of his fingertips. Mesmerized, I did not realize that the program assistant, a girl who lived near me, had returned from her errand and was attempting to get my attention. Our eyes met, and she waved.

I grasped the door handle and walked in.

"Good morning," I said. "I was just—"

"Hi, Em!"

Her voice was cheery and her face round and bright. "How are you, Kristi? It shouldn't be that we see each other only at school."

"I know. Crazy." She shrugged her shoulders. "We're like, what? Two doors down. Hey guess what? Danny and I are getting married!"

She stretched out her left hand.

"It's beautiful. Congratulations," I said, inspecting the diamond. "When is the wedding?"

"This spring. Next spring! Oh, you know what I mean. March!" She laughed and turned pink in the face, her shiny dark hair swishing about her shoulders.

"Oh how wonderful. Will you have it in Copper Bluff?"

"Yep, at St. Agnes. You'll come?"

"I wouldn't miss it," I said. "I'll mark my calendar."

"Tell me about the rest of your calendar, Em. Is March filling up already?" André said from his desk. His fingers kept pounding away at the keyboard, and his eyes never left the screen.

"God no. I've got nothing except the occasional committee meeting and academic conference," I replied.

"And those can be easily skipped, no?" he asked.

"I must admit, I'm not known for keeping *every* appointment, especially the small inconsequential ones the university would bog us down with if we would allow them ..." I hesitated.

He stopped typing momentarily and looked at me with his deep brown eyes, his shaggy brows lifted slightly. "Your annual review, was it not consequential?"

"I didn't miss that ... I was late. My cat got sick. Remember?"

Kristi nodded. "Yep, I do. You thought Mrs. Gunderson on the corner poisoned your cat because your cat bit her dog."

"Ah," André said.

"Mrs. Gunderson is a hostile woman and very territorial. It may sound improbable, but I know. I *know*." I suddenly felt hot and agitated. The whole conversation brought back memories I would have rather forgotten.

Now André leaned back in his chair. "Let us not think of that unpleasantness. Let us think of March ... in Paris." He closed his laptop with a click. "Over the summer, I applied for a grant to take our French students to Paris over spring break. I, of course, will need one more French teacher, and that teacher will be you."

Paris. André. André and I in Paris. It hardly seemed possible. "What do you mean, 'our French students'? What students?"

"The sixteen students I have right here on my roster." He held up a printout of his schedule. "And who knows? More might add this week," he said.

"Sixteen, well. Sixteen, that is wonderful." I began to get

excited. "How can you be sure they will want to go abroad?"

"Especially after all the violence over there," Kristi added, settling into her chair. "Parents might be too scared to let their kids go."

"It will be a concern, certainly, but now more than ever we must stand by our countrymen. We must not let terrorists dictate the future of the young minds. Don't you agree, Emmeline?"

I nodded. "Completely. If we can convince their parents, I will be the first one on the plane."

Visiting France was a lifelong dream of mine, students or no students. My great-great-grandma had been born in the small village of Saint Emilion, France; that was all I knew about her for certain. My mom claimed she was a poet; my dad insisted she was a potato farmer. Her history—albeit sketchy—spurred my love of France at a very young age. I imagined her life had been very different from mine, and at the age of ten, that was all it took to make it attractive.

"When will you find out about the grant?" I asked.

"Soon," he said. "Two weeks, perhaps. Spring does not seem so very far away, no?"

Spring, I silently repeated. Outside, the leaves were beginning to curl. Spring had never sounded so far away.

Chapter Three

———

I ENJOYED SEPTEMBER because students were at their most diligent. They attended lectures, they took notes, they called during office hours. The same could not be said for spring. The magic of fall had something to do with being gone and coming back. It affected the professors as well, including myself. Perhaps the students' eagerness propelled my own, or perhaps the humid days of July had become monotonous without the wonder of new faces. Whatever it was, I felt consumed by the *esprit* of the moment: labeling folders, sharpening pencils, reworking lesson plans—all on Friday afternoon.

I was posting my office hours, complete with a new motivational quote from Ralph Waldo Emerson, on my door when I saw Lenny locking up for the day. His office was directly across from the office of Barb, the secretary.

"Done for the day?" I called to Lenny.

"Yeah," he said, taking long strides toward my door, where he stopped to read my sign.

"What's this?" he asked. "Jeez. You don't actually tell them when you're going to be here, do you? Oh and Emerson. I should have known. I keep telling you you're a transcendentalist at heart. You won't listen. Still stuck on the French. What do they have for literature? *The Hunchback of Notre Dame*?"

"*The Hunchback of Notre Dame*? Really, Lenny—"

"Oh cool it. You know I'm just kidding you."

I knew he was, yet he still unnerved me every time with his uncanny ability.

"This is smaller than I remember," he said, walking into my office. "What did you do to get put in the closet anyway? You never told me."

I squeezed by him and sat down at my computer, closing my open program. "You're just not used to spending any time in your office."

He picked up the soft-cover book lying on my chair and sat down. "*Wuthering Heights*?"

I shrugged my shoulders. "I like something eerie in the fall."

He tossed it carelessly on the table. "What you need, then, is a little Washington Irving. 'Sleepy Hollow.' It's a good fall read."

"How is it, Lenny, that you always presume to know what I need when, in all accounts, it is exactly the opposite?"

When he didn't answer, I pushed away from my desk. "Of course, a headless horseman always makes for a curious read and certainly falls into the eerie category."

He stopped looking at my bookshelves and smiled. "So what are we doing?"

"Well, I don't know about you, but I'm finishing Monday's lesson plan."

He laughed, a deep sound that simply bounded off my four small walls. "I'm saving that for Sunday night. Come out with Claudia and me. She's reciting 'The Wolf' at Café Joe. Then some of us might meet up afterwards."

"Again, 'The Wolf'? Why not something else?" The thinly veiled poem, which I had heard no less than five times, was about Gene—Claudia's husband—and his wandering eye. The man was so dense that he had managed to sit through each reading and remark on the poem's beauty and rhythm. He never once caught Claudia's teeth gritting every time she said the word *prey*. The idea of hearing it again was as unpalatable as Barb and her Dixie cups.

Lenny threw up his hands. "Who knows? Maybe it's her favorite."

"I suppose," I said. "But I just drank an espresso—"

"You know, I think attendance is required? We actually got an email on it."

"Encouraged is not the same as required," I said, recalling the email. "But I think you're right. It's part of the back-to-school poetry slam going on tonight and tomorrow. I forgot all about it."

He raised his eyebrows. "Does that mean you're in?"

"Of course. I'll meet you there in an hour."

BECAUSE THE EVENING was mild and my inclination varied, I decided to walk to Café Joe. I stopped at my house only long enough to change into a pair of jeans and low-heeled boots. My purple short-sleeved shirt I kept on, tossing a jacket into my bag in case I stayed longer than I intended. It certainly was a possibility whenever Lenny was around.

"I won't be long," I said to my cat, Dickinson, who lay sleeping in the large bow window in my dining room. She didn't bother to open her eyes, but she did stretch her calico legs, knocking down a few journals I had stacked in the corner.

"Don't worry about those. I'll get them later," I told the cat, shutting the front door behind me.

I could hear the strains of a saxophone coming from the musical shrine on campus that housed several instruments considered relics. On Friday evenings, the shrine offered campus musicians opportunities to play near the fountain in front of the building; many of the compositions were classical, but a few were alternative or jazz.

A high-pitched bark interrupted the mellow little rift, and I didn't need to look to know where it came from. It was Mrs.

Gunderson's Darling, a small white mutt she walked up and down the street three times a day.

"Hello, Emmeline," Mrs. Gunderson said as Darling stopped to pee next to my pine tree.

I walked down my steps. "Hello."

"Nice out tonight," she said.

"Yes, it is." I kept my answers short, a lesson I'd learned the hard way when I'd found myself in the middle of an argument between her and Mrs. Walker, another neighbor.

"Are you going out this evening?" She raised her wrinkled blue eyelids as I walked toward her. Her mass of gray hair was meticulously curled and her pink lipstick neatly applied. She looked grandmotherly and kind, but after the incident with Dickinson, I knew she was capable of much darker deeds than making cookies.

"Yes, for a while. Goodnight, Mrs. Gunderson."

"Have fun, dear," she called behind me.

All the streets around campus were named for famous universities that little resembled our own. I lived on Oxford Street, exactly four blocks long. But those four blocks were populated with a multitude of personalities: there were the old ladies, conversant in all things holy; the students, willing to share anything from their views on politics to their beer bongs; and the teachers, who were happy to discuss all topics remotely related to their fields of expertise.

The husband and wife psychologists next to me were the most fascinating people on the block, at least to me. They were true artists, and never did I leave their presence without letting something slip that I wished I hadn't. They added these little tokens to my file, I felt, and each month it grew and grew until one day I was certain they would call a meeting to reveal exactly how much I had bungled my life.

I walked faster now, putting some distance between me and Mrs. Gunderson while still enjoying the assortment our street had to offer. All of the houses were old, but otherwise dissimilar. The students' houses were distinctively shabbier, their porches crooked with wood rot and dotted with threadbare sofas. Laughter and music and smoke tumbled from the houses, and it was no surprise to be awoken at two or three o'clock in the morning by a car horn or radio. Still, the noise was never angry; it was always playful and kind and easy to dismiss. Thus, it never became a problem, even for the elderly, who themselves kept odd schedules.

I reached the intersection of Main Street and Oxford, which didn't require a stoplight, and followed Main Street downtown. Copper Bluff was a pretty little town, built upon an orange-colored ridge for which it was named. Originally, the town had been located next to the reddish-colored river below the bluff, but after it flooded, the residents decided to pick up and rebuild it atop the bluff. The story of the town impressed upon me the meaning of pioneer spirit, for it embodied all that I knew about the place and the people. They persevered without complaint or question. It was never a matter of *if* something could be done but *how*.

Several of the old buildings had been preserved, several not. The downtown was a combination of the old, the renovated, and the happenstance. Café Joe was in a prime corner location, with large windows on both sides of the façade. Little bistro tables with padded chairs dotted the front of the coffee house while a few larger booths took up the space near the cash register. Besides hosting poetry readings, Café Joe also sold pottery and paintings, coffee beans and tea leaves, and chapbooks and CDs produced by local artists. It was considered a general meeting place for anything going on outside the campus that didn't include beer. What I liked about Café Joe was that it didn't have the pungent aroma of the chain-variety coffee shops; instead, it smelled of old books, damp rugs, and strong coffee.

Many English faculty, as well as two professors from Women's Studies, were already seated in a cluster of chairs facing the podium. Ann Jorgenson waved at me, and I started off in her direction. Ann taught a few cross-listed classes for us, since Women's Studies didn't offer enough courses to keep her busy most semesters. We became fast friends last spring when she taught Women Writers of the Twentieth Century, a class I'd taught several times and so could share notes.

"It's so good to see you!" Ann said as I approached her chair. She was wearing a short navy jacket that accentuated her tall frame and long legs, and her flat-ironed hair was perfectly highlighted blonde from root to tip. I silently reminded myself to make a hair appointment.

"Hi, Ann. How was your summer?"

"We had such a good time, didn't we?" she said, elbowing her husband, Owen, who taught Earth Science. She and Owen had been married five years but didn't have any children, despite their many attempts. This confidence Ann shared with a grin one afternoon while picking my brain about Virginia Woolf.

"We went to Hawaii to study rock formations—well, that's what Owen did," Ann said with another playful nudge. "I went to learn how to surf but became a pretty good boogie boarder instead. Have you ever tried that? Boogie boarding? It's a blast."

"No," I said, swallowing a white lie. I had tried to boogie board once on a trip to California and aspirated so much salt water that I had to be taken directly to the emergency room. It seemed there was no sport that I could not turn into a cautionary tale.

"She was a natural," Owen said with pride. He was not quite as good-looking as Ann, but his face was sincere and his smile genuine. His shoulders were straight and his arms muscular. I guessed he was one of those men who would maintain his athleticism well into middle age.

"How was your summer?" Ann asked.

I smiled. "It was rather quiet and peaceful and lost over the pages of several books. I read a fascinating tale of—"

Claudia Swift, one of our creative writing teachers and

editor-in-chief of *Copper Bluff Review*, called out Ann's name and pointed to her watch.

"Shoot, we'll catch up another time. I'm kind of running this thing tonight, you know," said Ann, quickly standing.

"We'll talk at the committee meeting for certain," I said.

She nodded briefly. "Yes. Next week." Then she was off to check the microphone and electrical equipment.

I said goodbye to Owen and moved toward an open chair near Claudia, who was busily scanning her poem, "The Wolf." I did not see her husband, Gene, and this was some recompense. When he was absent, Claudia told the most captivating stories about their marriage and two children. She was a terrific storyteller, and I could see why the creative writing students admired her, despite her mediocre poems.

"Hi, Claudia," I said, sitting down on the small wooden chair. "I heard you're reading tonight."

Claudia ran her fingers through her straight brown hair, giving it a little shake around her shoulders. This habit of hers usually ended in her fashioning it into a makeshift French twist by the end of the evening.

"*Em.*"

She said my name with such emphasis that I leaned in closer.

"I'm so glad you're here. Your support, *everyone's*, it's just phenomenal. Gene and I had an argument—on the way out the door—and my nerves are in tatters. That man has no conscience, none whatsoever. Of course he knows I'm moderating tonight, with Ann's help. He doesn't care; it doesn't stop him." She took a breath and reached for my hand, clasping it briefly. "But how are you? You look wonderful. Your eyes are positively *indigo* in that shirt. We have to talk about the fall issue of the *Review*. The galleys were less than perfect and now I have twenty divas breathing down my neck. Morgan's new. She's nineteen. What can I say? Our budget … oh god. I'm up."

With that she stood, smoothing her black dress and adjusting an aqua-blue scarf that flowed all the way down her back. Ann gave her a thumbs up, and Claudia briskly approached the microphone.

"Poets, students, colleagues, *friends*," she began. "We're here tonight as a community brought together by a common love: poetry."

Claudia's voice was barely above a whisper yet rose higher and lower at just the right intervals to give it a beautiful singsong quality. The effect was terrific, so much so that several times I caught my head bobbing to the rise and fall of her voice. I took a break from listening to Claudia and scanned the group nonchalantly. I spotted Lenny, who winked.

"'The Wolf,'" Claudia said, her voice a low hiss.

I listened as intently as I could, knowing that she often revised this poem and expected me to notice each time with my "keen ear." Although I was not a creative writer, she confused me for one because of my work as assistant editor of the *Copper Bluff Review*. In reality, Giles had promised to lighten my teaching load in return for my editorial skills, and I eagerly agreed. It was a position the other creative writing teacher, Allen Dunsbar, should have filled, but he was known for being lazy and generally unorganized. In fact, since publishing his second novel and receiving tenure, he'd become almost unbearable. Unlike Claudia's students, his students had nothing good to say about him. He was not even in attendance tonight. Typical Dunsbar.

Claudia finished "The Wolf" (with only one small addition of a red-headed beauty) to the sound of hearty applause, and I seized the opportunity to order a cappuccino. As I stood near the register, waiting for the new cashier to figure out the frothing machine, I examined the pottery on the counter, picking up a rainbow mug with the words "Be Colorful" etched on it.

"Frankly, my dear, I don't give a damn if you buy another coffee cup. Just don't buy another one with a cutesy slogan," said Lenny in his best Clark Gable imitation.

I put down the cup. "Dunsbar didn't bother to show up. Did you notice?"

"Yeah. What a punk. Half his students are here."

The cashier handed me a tiny white cup with foam oozing onto its saucer. Then she abruptly took it back and shook something that looked like nutmeg on the top.

"There," she said, thrusting it back into my hand.

"I'll just take a … coffee—black," said Lenny.

A boy wedged in the corner caught my eye.

"What is it, Prather?" Lenny took a sip of his coffee. "Damn, that's hot."

"That gentleman over there—he's my student." I motioned toward the corner with my chin.

"You mean that kid over there in the black cap? So? So what?"

"His name," I said quietly, "is Austin Oliver. And he dislikes poetry."

Lenny shrugged his shoulders. "Maybe he's here with some girl. That's how I got into this gig in the first place."

I shook my head, confused. "Are you telling me you got your PhD in literature because of some girl? Never mind. Tell me later. The point is Austin wanted to drop my class on Monday because one of the requirements is to recite a poem."

"You should be ashamed of yourself, Em. You've probably frightened the poor kid half to death, and he's scared as shit to get up there in front of the class and read a poem."

I stirred my cappuccino. "No, that's not it. He doesn't strike me as the timid type."

"You give people too much credit," said Lenny. "My bet is still on some girl. Girls are powerful at that age."

"Girls are powerful at any age. Come on," I said, noticing Giles looking in our direction. "Let's get back."

The poems were diverse, dramatic, and some, downright dreadful. Soon I forgot all about Austin Oliver. Claudia captivated me with a tale about the recent argument with her husband, which, from what I could decipher, was about his mother and whether or not she'd called Claudia "reckless" during one of their telephone conversations. Although reckless was an adjective that adequately described Claudia, mainly because of her penchant for drama, I kept this opinion to myself. Lenny, however, told her there was no doubt in his mind Gene's mother had called her reckless, and furthermore being reckless was nothing to be ashamed of. She nearly kissed him when he imparted this nugget of wisdom, and so pleased was he with himself, his company became nearly intolerable afterward. The proverbial straw, however, came when he turned to me keenly and said, "And there, Em, goes your student with his arm around some girl. I hate to say I told you so, but you know that I did."

Chapter Four

OVER THE WEEKEND, I realized Lenny was probably right; he usually was when it came to the many things I found mysterious. He once said I treated every encounter like a scene from a novel, placing it neatly on an invisible plot line that ran through my head. Plotline or not, I had to mention the poetry slam to Austin before class today. I needed to know why he attended.

Staring at my coffee pot made it brew no more quickly, so I checked my front stoop for the Monday newspaper. Not surprisingly, the porch was bare. I leaned over the railing and found the paper thrown between the hostas and the front steps.

"Hey, Professor Prather!" a voice hollered.

I straightened up, and an unexpected dizziness filled my ears. I cursed Lenny for persuading me to go to O'Malley's for Sunday night twofers. I couldn't resist its tap beer and cheap jukebox, and he knew it.

I squinted, readjusting my glasses, and realized a group of students was hailing me from across the street.

"Good morning," I said with an enthusiastic wave. My robe dropped open to reveal unmatched pajama tops and bottoms with cats and miniature Eiffel Towers, respectively. Several snorts followed in my direction, and I ducked back inside the safety of my home.

Built in 1917, my house had rich walnut woodwork and sturdy oak floors. The main room consisted of a living room and dining room with a pair of walnut-pillar bookshelves dividing the large room in half. Off the main room were two small bedrooms with large windows and sills where my cat, Dickinson, lounged on warm afternoons. One of the bedrooms was to be used as my study, but I often did my work in the dining room, which had a large rectangular table, good for holding stacks of folders and books. It also had a lovely bow window and a bench—the perfect vantage point for admiring my rose bushes and Arc de Triomphe replica bird feeder.

The coffee machine beeped, and I returned to the kitchen. The rich aroma filled the room, only big enough for a small round table, where I placed the morning's newspaper, and two hard-backed chairs. I poured the coffee into a white mug and drank it standing up, thinking about nothing in particular except the warmness of the day and the persistence of the wind. Then I poured a second mug and set it on the table while I looked for my apricot jam. There was a wonderful bakery eleven miles away that made delectable croissants, buttery and flaky. They went perfectly with apricot jam.

I sat down at the table with a croissant, enjoying the sun stretching into the kitchen window. Dickinson sat in the chair opposite me, glowering at my croissant until eventually she became irritated and bounded off the chair and through the doorway in one fluid motion. This was fine with me, since I didn't particularly enjoy seeing and hearing her tongue while I ate breakfast, especially with a mild hangover. I stretched my feet onto the empty chair, sipping my second cup of coffee in silence.

After breakfast and a hurried shower, I made my way to campus. It was Week Two, but my morning composition class remained diligent. This section had been especially punctual, which would probably change as the weeks waned into months. Today I was the punctual one, fifteen minutes early, stacking my handouts into neat little piles, according to their distribution, and writing the day's agenda on the chalkboard in the best cursive handwriting I could muster.

I heard someone enter the room as I finished writing on the board. Then, laying down the chalk and dusting off my hands, I looked up to see Austin Oliver. He wore a T-shirt and jeans, and he took his English folder and notebook from his backpack. He slouched into his desk in the back row and stared at his closed notebook. His indifference was an act; he was trying very hard to fit in with university life.

"Hello, Austin," I said.

He looked up as if he hadn't noticed I was in the room. "Oh, hi."

"Did you have a nice weekend?"

He nodded. "It was all right, I guess."

"What did you think of the poetry slam?" I said, writing the date in my grade book. It took him a moment to answer, and I knew the question had surprised him.

"It was okay," he said.

I looked up. "Some of those students were quite good, wouldn't you agree? That redhead, Sam … I taught him last year. He wrote very comical essays."

He shrugged. "I don't remember."

"Really?" I said. "The gangly redhead with the poems chock full of explicit language?" Now I suspected him of being difficult.

"I'm sorry. I don't remember any specific poems."

"Well. Poetry readings are excellent places for meeting girls." For some reason, this sounded borderline inappropriate. His blank face confirmed my suspicions, and I desperately tried to come up with a way to rephrase the statement but couldn't.

"I'll keep that in mind," he managed.

Jared Johnson, the well-dressed wisecracker who sat next to Austin, burst into the room with another of the boys from the back row, and I reluctantly moved to the podium.

Jared beat on the desk with his large fists as he passed. "Hey, brother. Are you ready to show your true devotion to the house?"

Austin leaned back in his chair. "I was born ready."

"Oh yeah, farmer?" he said, kicking Austin's boot, which protruded into the aisle. "That's what moron here said last year, and he puked five times."

"Once! I puked once," said Adam Norris, the other boy in the back row.

"You puked once in front of me and four times in front of the others," said Jared. "That makes five, last time I checked."

"Well, I'm here, aren't I?" said Adam, taking his book out of his backpack and carefully opening to a color-tabbed page. "And lucky for you that I am."

"Yeah, yeah. You make us look good," said Jared.

At this, they all laughed, a sound that didn't express appreciation, and I quit listening. What they were discussing I had heard discussed several times over and with the same sick feeling in my stomach: rush week, a time for students to rush campus fraternities and sororities for possible membership. Our fraternity and sorority inductions were mild compared to such rituals happening on other campuses. Still, last year a boy had to be taken to the hospital after drinking ten tequila shots, and another left town altogether after walking into a retirement home, completely naked, during bingo hour. Such hazing was thoughtless and irresponsible, and any time I could tell one of the members what I thought, which was frequently, I did. Now, however, was not the right time, especially with the last students filing into their seats. I opened my book, and the class fell silent.

After class, I stopped at Austin's desk.

"You know, Austin," I said, "I was thinking that if you found a poem you enjoyed during the poetry slam, you could recite it for class. I wouldn't be averse to allowing an unpublished poem to be recited for credit."

"That's a good idea, but I can't think of one that stood out," he said, hoisting his backpack over his shoulders.

"Not one?" I asked.

He shook his head.

"Or if there is a friend's poem you like? I will accept that for the assignment."

His tanned face turned just pink enough to tell me he was embarrassed.

So Lenny was right. It was about the girl.

"Forgive me for intruding. I just don't want you to worry about Friday's assignment. That's why I'm asking about the poetry reading," I said.

He brushed off my apology with a shake of his head. "I have to admit that I'm not looking forward to it, but I'll get through it. You get used to doing stuff you don't like to do on a farm," he said.

"So you did move from a farm." Most times, my first impressions were spot on. I congratulated myself for yet another. "How do you like the big city?" I asked.

He smiled. "Even people around here act like a farm is another planet."

I nodded. "Still, I don't meet many kids from local farms. I suppose it has something to do with corporate farms buying up the small family farms? I don't know exactly."

"My dad—well, he's not my real dad—is selling our farm. My parents are getting a divorce."

"I'm sorry to hear that," I said. About a third of my students wrote about their parents' divorce, and I was always saddened by the many ways it affected them.

"It's fine. Or it will be when I find something else to do with my life," he said. "I just wish I'd have studied a little harder in high school, if you know what I mean."

I knew the last thing he wanted was my pity, but I couldn't help but feel sorry for him. Even at this young age, he could have his dreams squelched by his parents' decision to divorce and sell the farm. But he would do well in school, and I told him so as I walked back to the podium. "You're a smart individual, Austin. You're doing just fine in this class—poetry or not— and you're going to do well in your other classes. I have every confidence in you."

"We'll see if you still think that after you read my paper," he said, heading toward the door.

We both laughed, and I felt a new trust that hadn't been there before.

"See you Wednesday," he said.

"I look forward to it," I replied.

After packing up my books and erasing the board, I hurried to avoid being too late to my meeting. Although much of my time was spent teaching, I also belonged to a multidiscipline committee charged with the welfare of the arts on campus. We met twice a month, and that morning was to be our first session of the year. I assumed the production of *Les Misérables* would be the focal point of our discussion, as it was the major artistic endeavor being undertaken this semester. I was thrilled with the selection, for it was one of my favorite works of French literature. I had read the eight-hundred page tome as a senior in college, and it had greatly influenced my application to graduate school. I couldn't wait to hear what the Theater Department had planned.

The meeting was to take place in Windsor, a terrific old building that was attached to my own Harriman Hall via a suspended passageway made out of frosted security block. I only had to step up from the English hallway and through the passageway to reach Windsor. My first semester at Copper Bluff, I taught in a room immediately following the walkway. I discovered that pigeons often got stuck in a small opening above and would beat their wings against the walls until they found their way out. It was an eerie sound, hard to dismiss. During a quiz or test, when the students were quiet, the sound grew disconcerting, if not downright debilitating. Walking through the passageway now, I realized no one would ever suspect such a thing could be true. It was completely silent.

Room 208 was located on the floor that housed both the History and the Women's Studies Departments. The Women's Studies Department was small and boasted only three faculty members, one being Ann Jorgenson, who was on the committee. Also in the group were two theater faculty, Alexander Schwartz, a perfectionist in every respect, and Dan Fox, Alex's go-to man and set designer. Rita Johnston, a surprising participant from Health and Wellness, was a mother of four and a champion chess player. I liked talking to her about vitamins and supplements and other cure-all pills that promised to improve or extend my life.

The committee members were seated near the front of the room—all except Alex, who stood at the whiteboard with his hands in his pockets, rocking back and forth on his heels. Alex was a heavy-set man with a barrel-shaped stomach and a bald head. His eyes and eyebrows were dark brown and his mouth so small that it became the focal point of his large, bland visage. Perhaps this is why people listened when he talked, even when he was wrong. The results of his work were beyond reproach, and I had a great deal of respect for him because he represented writers so well.

Dan Fox was a much smaller man but no less important, of that I was sure. He seemed the consummate dreamer, forever gazing out windows and speaking too softly. His mousy brown hair hung straight in his face and always seemed in need of a good clipping. Despite their odd-couple appearances, however, I predicted that they worked well together, as is often the case when balance is paramount to the success of a project.

Rita and Ann sat to the left of the podium, several chairs away from Dan, and I took one of the empty chairs near them.

Rita had beautiful red hair, wavy and smooth and cut nicely above the ears. One would guess by her hair that she was several years younger than she truly was. Ann was a few years older than I was but probably had a hard time being taken seriously by her students because of her extraordinary good looks. As I sat down beside her, I noticed that her clothes always hung as they did in fashion magazines. Mine nearly did—with the help of a sturdy pair of control tops and three-inch heels.

"The poetry slam was a hit last Friday," I whispered. "Everyone had a great time."

"I thought so, too," said Ann. "Quite a few people showed up."

Just then Jane Lemort entered, and my heart sank. After learning that one of the committee members would be on sabbatical this semester, she'd asked me about his replacement, but I'd stayed as vague as possible. I knew she was just fishing for some new way to appear *involved*—as if her membership in twelve other groups and chapters meant nothing. She was obsessed with being well-known on campus; she thought it tantamount to receiving tenure. Now here she was in all her medieval glory. We smiled at each other cordially, and she took the seat next to mine, commenting on my "interesting" earrings. "Interesting" from her was another way of saying, "I wouldn't be caught dead in those."

"It's so nice to have the input of so many experts on my play," Alex said, immediately drawing murmurs from each of us insisting that we were not experts. "Oh don't worry. I'm not going to quiz you … at least not until the end of the meeting."

We all laughed.

"It's been a long summer, hasn't it? I can't wait to sink my teeth into something substantial," said Alex.

"You can't get more substantial than *Les Mis*," said Rita.

Alex nodded. "It's going to present certain challenges, that's for sure. I, for one, am not looking forward to the slaying of some of the musical numbers." He shuddered. "It will take time. But I have every confidence in our student body. Sarah sung very nicely for the part of Fantine," he said with a nod in my direction.

I leaned back. I knew Sarah from last year's *Brigadoon*, but I couldn't recall if she was in English. She must have been.

"Sarah is such a nice girl and a gifted creative writer," Jane interjected.

I wanted to roll my eyes but refrained. I couldn't imagine a medievalist would have any opinion whatsoever on modern creative writing.

"Jane! Welcome," said Alex. "Forgive me for not introducing you to the rest of the group. This is Jane Lemort from English. You probably know everyone already."

"Mostly," she said, glancing around the room. "And thank you. I'm glad to be here."

"*Les Mis* feels so right this year; wealth inequality is being discussed in a lot of classrooms," I said, returning to the play. "I cannot wait to see what you come up with for the set."

"Two years ago I saw it performed in New York, and they made a towering replica of the barricade," said Dan. "That's what I have in mind."

"Oohh," said Ann. "I like the sound of that."

Alex looked agitated. "Nothing has been agreed on yet, though."

"Oh no, of course not," said Dan, completely noncommittal. His passion seemed to deflate with each poke of Alex's serious voice.

"But whatever we choose, we'll need several dozen volunteers to get it right," continued Alex. "The set will be a huge undertaking but well worth the effort. What do you think about extending a little extra credit in your classes?"

At this, we chuckled. Extra credit came in quite handy when it came to finding volunteers.

"I have three new freshmen this year and—you won't believe

this—one fellow is quite strong, a bona fide farmhand!" said Dan.

"Ah … a thespian of the first tier," said Alex.

These were exactly the kind of comments that made me critical of Alex. He could be so condescending.

"Actually, he's pumped about the work. I think you know him, Emmeline. He said he's one of your students. Austin something-or-other."

"Austin Oliver?" I asked, surprised.

"Yeah, that's it." Dan swept his shaggy hair from his eyes. "Nice kid. Likes the theater, I guess. I talked him into taking Theater Appreciation next semester, so at least we'll have him around for a couple of semesters."

"Smart thinking," said Alex. "We always need a guy like that around—if for nothing more than brute strength."

Now I *was* irritated. I certainly would not stand for anyone putting down a student of mine. "I'm sure he'll prove useful in more ways than one. I've found Austin to be a very intelligent young man with many talents. He's much smarter than that clod who played Mr. Darcy … what was his name? Derrick? Drake?"

"Daniel," ground out Alex.

I dismissed him with the wave of my hand. "Of course, *Daniel*. Hardly believable in that part."

Ann covered her mouth and coughed.

"I have an event," Jane interceded, perhaps on my behalf, "that I'd like us to promote. I'm partnering with the Music Department to bring Medieval Music Mondays to our sack lunch program. Every Monday in the month of October, there will be live medieval music and poetry at the Music Museum."

I wasn't certain what kind of music was played in medieval times, but all I had to do was picture Jane with a lyre, and the program became intolerable.

"I like it," said Rita. "Nobody knows a damn thing about anything further back than the War of 1812. At least I don't."

Rita had a point. The program might help demystify Jane's very existence.

"I was hoping we could advertise it on public radio—just through September—to get off on the right foot," she said.

"Oh I don't know, Jane. That's a lot of money spent on something that doesn't generate any revenue," said Alex.

Although I thought advertising the program on public radio was a bit overzealous, I didn't appreciate Alex's newly asserted dictatorship. He had no more power than Jane did when it came to deciding what events we would create and promote. "Careful, Alex. You sound suspiciously like the Athletic Department," I said.

Now his tiny mouth formed a smile. "Oh god, we can't have that." He closed his notebook and relaxed his shoulders. "I'm sorry, Jane. I think it's a great idea. I really do. Budget cuts make it harder and harder every year to allocate funds appropriately."

"That's because there are no funds," said Ann. "I think it's ludicrous what this university expects us to make do with so little."

We all nodded vaguely in agreement. In some ways, Ann was right. She was an up-and-comer in an up-and-coming field. She had ideas she couldn't possibly put into action on such a small campus. For scholars like me, however, who were connected to the past as if by an invisible string, this campus was ideal. We didn't need or want much to change, and lack of funds ensured nothing much did.

After the meeting, I took the main staircase that led outdoors instead of the passageway because it was ten minutes to the hour, and following Alex's extended harangue on the financial future of the arts, I longed for the rash vernacular of the student body brushing up against me. Hearing them shout to their friends, eating sandwiches and drinking sodas, conjugating Spanish verbs … it was all a part of something that I loved absolutely. I stood in the hallway, unmoving, listening and hoping never in my lifetime to cease understanding what it meant.

The crowd thinned, and I was left with nothing but an empty hallway and an empty feeling in my stomach. I prided myself on knowing my students. Even if I didn't remember their names, I always remembered their stories. I began to write them down long before they wrote their first papers, and I suppose, in that respect, I *was* a bit of a storyteller, perhaps one who had lost her touch. Austin Oliver, after all, contradicted each new page that I wrote.

Chapter Five

———

AT THE END of the week, my composition students were to begin reciting their poems. They had had almost two weeks to select a poem, and I arrived early on campus Friday morning in anticipation. Sometimes students would drop by my office before class, asking about a pronunciation or the meaning of a word or phrase. Such thoroughness was rare, but it satisfied me to know that some students took their assignments seriously.

Barb was already in and so was Giles, and that meant that the coffee was brewed. I rummaged through the bottom of my book bag, searching for spare change. All I had were several pennies. I casually glanced back at the door to make sure no one was watching. Then I dropped three pennies in the can and filled my to-go mug.

I surreptitiously backed out of the door, zipping my bag with one hand and holding my coffee with the other. I made one bold move into the hallway and toward my office door, a small smile of triumph on my lips. My smile faded, however, as I realized I didn't have my office key in hand. I quickly reopened my bag.

I heard footsteps and was certain they were Barb's, the coffee can open, the thief revealed. But they were not Barb's. To my surprise they belonged to Austin Oliver, walking down the hallway as if he were lost.

"Austin!" I called out. He froze for a moment but did not turn around. "Austin!" I said again. Now he turned and squinted. I waved. He started walking in my direction. "I'm glad I caught you," I said. "I just got here. Come in, come in."

I threw my bag on the table and sprung open the shade. Then I plopped down in my office chair and motioned to the other chair for him to do the same. He did not. Clad in light blue jeans and a flannel shirt, he stood awkwardly, glancing around the small room.

"So, which poem did you decide on? Or did you come to see if I would make good on my bet?" I asked. "It's rather last minute, but no one could accuse me of shirking a duty."

He continued to examine my office with interest. He squinted at some of the titles of my books, even going so far as to take one out and frown at it.

"Hmm?" he said.

I smiled. "That's a first edition of Whitman. A history professor gave it to me as a graduation present. Did you choose a Whitman poem?" I pulled my battered text out of my bag and began thumbing through it.

Now he turned and looked at me, and I could see he was under duress. His eyes seemed larger, and I decided this was because he was not smiling. He was again the unsure student from the first day of class. Maybe Lenny was right. Maybe he really *was* worried about reciting the poem. Still, I couldn't help but wonder if something else were on his mind.

"It is the poem, isn't it?" I asked. "You did come to see me about the poem?"

He stared at me quizzically, perhaps wondering if I could be trusted with a secret. Many students had looked at me in this same way, hoping to find a sympathetic ear on the other side.

For a moment, I thought he would tell me about the girl in the parking lot, confide in me that he was in danger. I touched the arm of the facing chair.

But he did not sit down. Instead, he straightened his shoulders and said, "Yes. 'Those Winter Sundays.' "

Now it was my turn to be at a loss for words.

"The poem I chose is 'Those Winter Sundays,' " he repeated.

"Yes ... well," I said, trying to regain my speech. "That is a fine poem. The word choice is simple; it has good alliteration. An important aspect of this poem, I guess, is how you view the speaker's feelings about his father."

"I don't know," Austin said, shifting his weight from foot to foot. "I guess he feels bad about the way he treated him."

I nodded encouragingly. "The tone is certainly one of regret. Dads perform a lot of tasks for which they aren't always thanked, wouldn't you say?"

He shrugged. "My dad—stepdad—he got up early like the dad in the poem. He did a lot of chores I never really appreciated when I lived on the farm. I suppose that's why he wants to sell it."

"Oh no," I said, my brow furrowing. "I'm sure it was a decision both your parents came to when they determined to divorce. It has nothing to do with you."

"That's what everyone says. But if that's true, why did they wait until now to tell me he wasn't my real dad?" There was anger as well as sadness behind his words.

"I'm sure they were waiting until they thought you were old enough to process the news; it was just bad timing with the divorce," I said carefully.

"Maybe. But if my dad really cared, why is he selling the farm? He knew I planned to farm; *we* planned on it since I was a kid. He didn't even give me a chance to make some money or get a loan to buy it. He wants to sell it immediately ... before he moves to Toledo. Where is that even at?"

"Ohio," I said automatically. His reaction told me he hadn't expected an answer.

"And now ... well, it doesn't matter." He coughed. "I've moved on. That's why I'm here, right?" His voice still held a good deal of uncertainty.

"You're absolutely right," I said. I didn't want to lose any of the ground I had gained. "You can find a new passion here. It could even be poetry."

Now he grinned, and I started to feel better about the direction of the conversation. The feeling, however, was short-lived.

"In fact, I just happen to have a recording of that poem of yours. I think you'd really enjoy hearing the author's rendition." I started to rifle through the stack of CDs near my computer.

"You know, Professor Prather, I think I'm good. I gotta get going," he said.

"Nonsense! We have at least thirty minutes before class," I said, digging faster.

"That's okay, really."

He was halfway to the door. I frowned, noticing that he wasn't toting his book bag.

"See you later."

"If you have to go ..." I said, trying to catch the CDs, now falling one after the other onto the floor. But it was too late— for him and the CDs. Both were out of my reach.

When I got to class that morning, I wasn't surprised that he was absent. He hadn't been carrying his book bag, after all. Maybe he hadn't planned on attending. Yet, as I stood staring at his empty spot, I began to worry about the unusual circumstances of the encounter. He had chosen a poem; he had come in to discuss it. Or had he wanted to discuss something else?

Chapter Six

—

On Sunday evening, Jim Giles's name appeared on my caller ID. He hadn't contacted me at home since my first day of teaching. Now I listened as a third party might while Giles told me a student of mine, Austin Oliver, had been found dead in the theater.

"Dead," I said to Giles, repeating the word into the receiver as if unfamiliar with its definition.

"Yes. He died working on the set of *Les Misérables* last evening. They found him this morning. I wanted you to hear it from me first …. I'm very sorry, Emmeline."

I moved a stack of books from my dining-room chair to the floor and slowly sat down. "What happened? Did he fall?"

"No, nothing like that as far as I understand," said Giles. "They are still determining what caused his death."

"They don't know?"

"They just found him this morning; they assume he died Saturday night. You know what a ghost town it is on the weekends. I mean, what I meant to say is, they *will* find out what happened. It looks very bad for the university until they do."

That was true. To have a student die on campus while working on a university project was bad news. President Conner was probably covering all angles and deciding the scenario that would look best for the university.

"Where was Alex? How could he have allowed something like this to happen?" I asked.

"I can't imagine Alex was involved," answered Giles. "And we don't know what was allowed and what wasn't."

"I can't imagine he *wasn't* involved. He can be found in anything that has to do with the theater." I stood up and pushed my dining room chair toward the hallway, where a package of cigarettes balanced on the wide casing of the linen-closet door. I had quit smoking years ago, but when the occasional urge to fail every one of my students or expatriate to France came upon me, a cigarette could still calm my nerves. I stood on tiptoe, feeling for the box with my fingertips, the phone crooked under my chin. The cigarette pack fell to the floor with a clunk.

"That doesn't necessarily constitute his guilt in the matter, Emmeline, although I know it would be easier for you to place the blame somewhere. The truth is accidents happen all the time. This time it happened to one of your students, and for that I'm truly sorry."

I found my kitchen matches, conveniently placed in the drawer next to the silverware and easily within my reach. I struck the box and lit my cigarette, inhaling deeply and tossing the pack onto the kitchen table.

"Emmeline?"

"I'm here," I said. "I know you're right. I just wish I could have left him on better terms. I don't think he liked my class."

"Oh. Well, I can't say if the word 'like' or 'dislike' really matters in this context. We're here to teach them something, aren't we? Sometimes they like what we're teaching; sometimes they don't. It doesn't mean he didn't like you. Besides, isn't he the one you were telling me about who came to your office on Friday?"

I sank into a kitchen chair. "Yeah," was all I could say, because I didn't want to admit to Giles I knew then that something was wrong. I could tell by the look on his face. The kid wanted a friend or someone to talk to. If only I could go back, if only I could have gone about our conversation differently … I wouldn't have started talking about the damn poem.

"See? He wouldn't have come if he completely despised you," said Giles.

"Well, that's true," I said.

"And so many of your students have extraordinary things to say about you at the end of the semester," he added.

"Thank you. I do feel better," I said.

"Good." Giles sounded relieved. "Now, get some rest tonight, and I'm sure we'll find out more tomorrow."

"Okay. Goodnight." I hung up the receiver.

Rest, however, would be elusive that evening; my mind was already anticipating the details that were sure to come to light in the next day or two. I took another drag of my cigarette and watched a curl of smoke dissipate into the recesses of the dark kitchen. It seemed impossible, but not surprising, that Austin was dead. He was one of those students who didn't exactly fit in, so if something were to happen to someone, it might be him. Of course what had happened was an accident; Giles had said so himself. Still, I wondered about the girl from the parking lot. Could she have had anything to do with his death?

My cigarette burned itself down to the filter. I rinsed it under the sink. Then I looked out the window for a long time. It was still light outside but just barely, the evening shadows wreaking havoc with the two-story Victorian on the corner. The tree branches seemed longer and sharper and the wind, brisker. It snaked between houses, found hordes of leaves, and threw them recklessly into the narrow street. Standing there, I realized we were all a little like those leaves, given to the caprice of outside forces, and suddenly life seemed more perilous. Had Austin not entered our town, entered our campus, entered our theater, he might be alive right now. What he would be doing, I didn't know. I felt as if everything I did know about him was either inconsistent or incomplete. Tomorrow, however, I would go about finding out everything I could, and what, if anything, I could have done to prevent his death.

Chapter Seven

———

THE NEXT MORNING was beautiful, the kind that makes you feel you have done something wonderful with your life just by waking up. The air was so cool that even the warm sun could not hide the fact that it was the third week of the semester, and September was coming to a close. A new urgency propelled the students' footsteps, making the campus feel abuzz with life and learning. It was hard to imagine that only two days ago, a student had died on this same campus. My student. I pulled my dark-green jacket tighter and walked quicker, ignoring the faint scent of honeysuckle as I passed by the old College of Law Building. It seemed unfair to partake in life's little joys when something so dreadful had just occurred.

Normally, Lenny didn't come to campus on Mondays; he claimed it was out of perpetual mourning for Sundays. So when I saw him, I knew he had heard about the death. It had, after all, been front-page news in *Plain Speak*, Copper Bluff's daily newspaper. Although it filled the front page, the article included few details about Austin's death, saying only that he had been working on the set of the university play and died "suddenly." It did, however, include an oversized photo of

Austin, standing next to a tree. Probably his senior picture.

"Em, wasn't that your student—" started Lenny.

"Yeah," I said.

"Come on," he said, walking toward Harriman Hall. "Let's talk in my office."

His office décor was a hodgepodge of everything from baseball memorabilia to Beatles posters to a fine painting of Walden Pond. He had an impressive collection of books, but unlike mine, his were neat and orderly and did not appear to have been read for some time—if ever. His desk was much larger than mine and offered more writing room, a coffee maker, and a laptop. I wondered how I had been on campus a year without the thought of buying a new computer entering my head. I still had an old Acer with a monitor as wide as my entire desk and a CD-ROM that didn't burn anything. I took what the college had given me because I didn't have the money or the inclination to invest in anything better. Yet I knew I would need to address my computer situation soon. So many of my students were engrossed in their smartphones during class, though, that I realized the harm an obsession with the latest technology could bring. It's not that I didn't own a smartphone—I did—I just went out of my way not to become dependent on it. In fact, I was one of the few young people I knew who still had and used a landline.

"I knew it was the same kid from the coffee shop. Want a cup? I charge just twenty cents."

I nodded. He was the only person in the world I knew who drank as much coffee as I did. He selected a filter from an enormous stack, heaping it with a massive scoop of coffee. Then he filled the coffee pot with a jug of filtered water, and we watched it brew in silence. As if observing an unwritten rule, we only began talking once it was finished.

He handed me a Dodger's cup that appeared as if it should have been thrown out ten years ago, but I said nothing. The coffee was quite good.

"What was he doing working on a play, anyway?" he asked. "He was no lover of poetry."

I started to answer and then stopped. I really didn't know the answer.

"Don't give me that screwy face," he said. "I'm sure you wonder as much as I do, especially since this kid wasn't exactly the artistic type."

"Well, of course I wonder as much as you do. I was his teacher!" I said.

"I know. Look, I'm sorry. I should have said that first."

I took another sip of my coffee. "I realize it's early in the semester, and I barely knew him, but he *was* my student, and I had concerns about him from the very beginning. You know I did."

"I know. That's why I asked about the play. It doesn't fit with what you told me," said Lenny.

"And there's something else ..." I said. I waited to make sure he was paying attention.

Lenny put down his coffee cup. "If you were going for a dramatic pause, I got it."

I spoke quietly. "The night of the potluck, I came to campus to pick up a few things from my office. When I got back to my car, I overheard an argument between a man and woman. Two students. I'm rather certain that one of them was Austin. The woman told Austin she could make his life a living hell."

Lenny leaned back in his chair. "How do you know it was Austin?"

It was so like Lenny to miss the important part of what I was saying. "Because of something he said to me the first day of class. He said that he *saw* me. From the parking lot. But the crucial point here is that he may have been in danger."

"From a girl? I don't know. I don't see too many dangerous girls roaming the campus."

I had to agree with him. "It may be nothing; I realize that."

"But you're right about one thing. A kid who doesn't like

poetry wouldn't go out of his way to work at a place that essentially does poetry on a larger scale. Maybe he signed up for extra credit?"

"No. He didn't. That's what makes it odd. Dan Fox said Austin signed up right away at the beginning of this semester."

Lenny tapped a pencil on his desk. "He didn't work in the theater last year?"

"He's a freshmen."

"Hmm. Well, maybe it doesn't matter that he was at the theater in the first place." He tucked the pencil behind his ear. "Maybe it has nothing to do with why he died."

I shrugged. "I suppose not. I just hate to leave questions unanswered, especially when it comes to one of my students."

"If I were you, I would talk to Dan. He'll tell you straight up what happened. More?" he asked, gesturing toward the coffee pot.

I nodded, and he poured us both another cup.

"That's a good idea. I think I'll go over there after class," I said.

"Let 'em out early," Lenny said. "I'll go with you. Isn't it student appreciation week or something?"

I laughed. "That was last week."

Someone tried Barb's door across the hall, and Lenny shouted out, "Barb's gone."

Giles poked his head through the door.

"Giles!" I said, putting down my coffee cup. "Have you heard anything else?"

Giles looked back and forth from Lenny to me and then walked into the office. "President Conner called me this morning. The police will be on campus today asking questions about Mr. Oliver."

"The police," I said, coming to terms with the situation in my head.

"They might even have some questions for you," Giles continued.

"For me," I repeated.

"Certainly," said Giles. "You were one of his teachers and probably one of the last people to see him alive."

The severity of the situation overcame me, and I could do nothing but stare back blankly at Giles, my head cocked in an unconvincing attitude of neutral curiosity.

Lenny reached over and patted my shoulder. "I believe what Giles is trying to say, Em, is that you are now officially under investigation."

I shrugged off his hand.

"Hardly," said Giles in his typical understated fashion. "Emmeline is no more under investigation than you or I. She just happens to be more directly involved because she was one of his professors."

"Still," I said, recovering the use of my vocal cords, "Lenny is right about one thing. They are performing an investigation, which means they must think it's possible that his death wasn't an accident."

"Oh I wouldn't go that far," said Giles. "They're not saying that someone killed him on *purpose*. They could be saying, though, that someone could be responsible for his death, and they are going to find out who."

Lenny looked in my direction. "That sounds like murder to me."

I raised my eyebrows.

Giles went over and slowly shut Lenny's door. "Listen, you two. Perhaps you enjoy reading mystery novels in your free time or watching old whodunits on A and E Sunday afternoons or just take pleasure in how the word rolls off your tongues, but here, on campus, with a serious investigation underway, please do not toss around the word 'murder' so lightly. In a department such as ours, susceptible to creative whims and make-believe, it's all the more important that we do not allow our imaginations to run away with us. Not only does it make us appear suspicious, it makes us look like crackpots."

"Crackpots, hah!" laughed Lenny. "Good one."

I shook my head.

"Just be careful, Emmeline," said Giles, more quietly. "You're in a fragile state right now and you might be prone to certain … activities that would not serve you or your student. I know you want answers; it's only natural. I want answers, and he wasn't even my student. Be patient and tolerant, and they will come. I will make certain of that."

I nodded, and Giles turned and opened the door. "We'll talk again. I have a class."

Lenny and I said nothing for several seconds. Then I turned toward Lenny.

"The theater building, one hour?" I asked.

"I'll be there."

THE ENTIRE CLASS was waiting for me attentively when I arrived, thinking I knew more than they did about Austin's death. In fact, I probably knew even less, since I hadn't read through the entire article in the newspaper because I awoke late after my sleepless night. When I placed my text on the podium, the sound echoed in the still silence of the room, and I stood for a long moment with my hands folded across the book, not knowing what to say. Of course, duty eventually overcomes all things, and I began to speak.

"I'm sure that most of you are aware that a classmate of yours, Austin Oliver, died on Saturday evening. He will be greatly missed in this classroom and on this campus. If you feel you need help coping with this situation, there is a free counseling service available to you, which is located in the Ronning Building—"

"Do you know what happened?" asked Adam. He sat in the back row with Jared, the other fraternity boy.

"No … not really," I said, still in a daze. Someone coughed. I turned from the window. "He was working on an upcoming play. He was found in the campus theater."

Adam looked at Jared, who shrugged.

"Did you have something you wanted to add, Adam?" I asked.

"No, we—I mean I—just didn't know he was into that. Theater."

"I think there was a lot more to Austin than any of us realized," I said. "Had we the time to plumb the depths of his mind, we might have been surprised."

I asked for a moment of silence in Austin's honor, and the class remained respectfully quiet. Then I opened my book, and a sigh of relief washed over the classroom. We were creatures of ritual, after all, all of us. It was nice to open a book and pretend that the troubles of the world outside could not and would not enter, even if they had once sat in the back row.

After class, I stopped at the water fountain. As I stood there, getting a drink, I saw Adam and Jared talking outside a deserted classroom. I hung back, sitting down on the bench beside the restrooms and looking through my bag as if I were searching for an item of the utmost importance.

Jared tossed his backpack over his one shoulder. "I told you he was a pussy."

"Being in a play doesn't make someone a pussy," said Adam.

"Yeah, well, it doesn't make him the tough SOB he acted like either," said Jared, zipping his gray fleece. "I guess he isn't so tough now." He started toward the stairs, with Adam following quickly behind.

I remained motionless for several moments, even after they had gone. I had a hard time liking that kid Jared. He was spoiled, arrogant, and predictable. There was a note of cruelty in nearly everything he said and wrote. It wasn't the typical freshmen chip on the shoulder. I had a sense it was something more, but he seemed to have everything he could desire. Young men flocked to him the same way they flocked to Worldwide Wrestling Federation. Perhaps they admired his courage, or perhaps they were shocked by his brazen antics. Whatever the reason, a group of students followed him wherever he went; he was rarely alone.

Adam was one of his groupies, certainly, but he was also a smart kid. I had a feeling that Adam did most of Jared's homework but did not write Jared's papers for one reason or another. Jared's essays could have used his help. He tutored him, according to what I had heard. Adam, perhaps, was brought into the fraternity for that very reason. Many students in fraternities and sororities had a grade-point average they needed to achieve to remain in the house. Sororities and fraternities adhered to certain academic rules and traditions that could not be broken without breaking the aura that surrounded them.

I stood and walked down the stairs, pausing momentarily near the Foreign Languages Department. I had no time to talk to André about the grant; I had to get to the theater. One of my students was dead, and I felt compelled to find out why.

Chapter Eight

—

W HAT WE CALLED the theater building was actually the Grant C. Hofer Center for the Fine Arts, which housed not only our campus theater but also the Art and Music Departments. It was a large brick building, across the street from the rest of the campus. A bronze sculpture of what looked like a hammer took up much of the lawn in front and blocked the main entry; one had to circle around it to enter the double doors. There were two other side entries as well, but the front entry allowed easiest access to the main theater, where the major productions were held. Down one hallway were pianos, trumpets, and violins. Down the other were drawings, paintings, and flyers advertising the services of nude models for art classes.

Lenny drove up in his aqua-blue Ford Taurus at the same time I was studying the hammer-like sculpture. I waited while he took his backpack out of the backseat and locked it in the trunk. Had I asked him what he was doing, he would have told me he didn't want his intellectual property stolen. Honestly, though, I wondered what he had in there that needed to be kept under lock and key.

"Hey," he said as he approached the building.

"What is this, anyway?" I asked, motioning to the sculpture.

"I don't know. A hammer?" He shrugged.

"I believe it's some sort of gavel," I said.

Lenny pushed open the front door to the theater and nearly collided with a man exiting.

"Excuse me," said the man.

That's when I realized it wasn't just any man: it was our newest faculty member. "Thomas Cook!" I exclaimed.

He stepped back, startled.

"Don't worry. She'll only call you by your full name for the first year or so," said Lenny.

Thomas smiled, calling attention to the deep middle part in his thick brown hair. He wore a dark suit jacket and an open-collared white shirt; his shoes were expensive—pointed and crocodile. His smile, his clothes, his demeanor—everything about him said *refined.*

"Ms. Prather. Forgive me for not remembering your first name. And Lenny, right?"

"It's Emmeline Prather and Lenny Jenkins," I said, smiling back at him. "What are you doing over here?"

His own smile grew comic. "I teach here, remember?"

Lenny laughed, but I had a feeling Cook was stalling.

When he realized I was still waiting for an answer, he said, "I'm still exploring the campus. I hadn't been to the theater yet, so I thought I would take the opportunity before my afternoon class."

"So you heard about that kid dying?" asked Lenny.

He looked from me to Lenny and nodded soberly. "Of course I read something about it in the newspaper. What a difficult way to begin the semester. But this is a lovely building with a terrific art department. Lydia will be delighted with the rotating exhibits."

"You didn't know the student then?" I asked.

He raised his eyebrows. "The student who died? No. Not

at all. I hardly know a soul on campus … except for English faculty."

I nodded.

"So what about you two? What brings you over here?"

I answered before Lenny could come up with an improbable excuse. "I'm on a committee with Alex Schwartz about *Les Mis*. It's the fall production."

Now he remembered. "Right. You're into French literature."

"Em is a serious Francophile. If you need to discuss anything related to scarfs or croissants, she's your gal," said Lenny.

Thomas smiled again and then placed his hand on the door handle. "I'll keep that in mind."

"Later," said Lenny.

I gave Thomas a small wave, and he was gone.

When the door had shut safely behind him, I turned to Lenny. "Well, that was odd."

"He's just as curious as we are but too cool to say so. Remember, Em, not everyone is as devious as they are in your chick lit novels."

I stopped. "You know I hate that word."

He smiled, showing his dimple. "Yeah, I know."

"In the 1920s, Virginia Woolf talked about our compulsive need to classify women's writing because it looks different than men's—and we're still doing it today. 'Chick lit.' 'Cozy'!" I huffed. "I swear, Lenny. I'm the only one writing about this in academia."

"Because you're the only one reading genre novels."

I truly doubted that statement. Lots of intellectuals needed the occasional escape from academia. But when they did, they didn't talk to me about it. My fondness for genre fiction was deeply rooted in my childhood in Detroit. From the time I learned to read, I turned to mysteries and romances as a way to flee the grim reality of city life. Among their pages, I found sympathy, justice, love, and hope.

"Come on, Susan B. Anthony," said Lenny. "You can

brainstorm your next conference paper another day. We're here to wage a different war."

We continued walking.

Immediately to the right was a large office with a receptionist. Behind her were two gray cubicles.

"Are you coming in?" I asked Lenny.

"I'll just wait out here," he said, studying the pictures on the walls of previous plays.

"Good morning," I said as I entered the room. "I'm looking for Dan Fox. Might you know where his office is?"

"I don't know if Dan really has an office, does he, Lori?" she said to someone behind a gray cubicle wall.

"No," a woman answered.

"I didn't think so. But he usually can be found in the costume shop or the theater if he's on campus," said the receptionist.

"Where is the costume shop?" I asked.

"Take your first set of steps on the left-hand side of the hallway," she said, pointing in the direction of the Art Department. "Go all the way down to the basement, through the hallway—there will be lots of crates—and knock on the door. It's always locked."

"Thank you," I said.

"I would try the theater first, though," said the unseen woman from the cubicle. "I think the police officers are still down there with Professor Schwartz."

"Oh, I bet you're right. Try the theater," said the secretary.

"Will do. Thank you," I said, immediately deciding I didn't want to miss the police interrogation, especially since it involved Alex.

"He doesn't have an office," I said to Lenny, "but the costume shop is this way."

Lenny slowly turned from the hallway pictures and began following me. "I was going to be in a play once."

"What happened?" I asked.

"My girlfriend broke up with me."

We entered the stairwell on the ground floor. Above and below us were concrete steps to the upper and basement floors. The fluorescent lights buzzed mechanically, flashing at unseemly intervals as we descended the stairs. I gripped the railing tightly as we went down two steep flights, my kitten heels making eerie music with each step. At the bottom of the stairwell was another metal door. I opened it, and after we passed through, it closed with an echo behind us.

Before us was a long hallway with rectangular containers lining its entire length. Some of the containers were open and contained fabric and rubber, hats and rugs, pillows and dishes. The costume shop was behind another door with pushbuttons for a code.

Lenny picked up a teapot. "What is all this? Props?"

"Shhh," I said. I could hear voices down the hallway.

"We're spies now? Is that it?" He put back the teapot.

"Listen, Officers, I understand that you have a job to do, and I respect it. I really do. But I have a job to do, too. I cannot have these delays take weeks instead of days, so do whatever it is that you have to do, and then get out."

The voice was unmistakably Alex's. I nodded at Lenny. He nodded back. Someone was heading our way. Lenny quickly picked up the teapot again.

"I think you're right. It was used in *My Fair Lady*," said Lenny in a poor British accent.

Alex rounded the corner and glared at Lenny, clearly annoyed by his unauthorized browsing. "Can I help you with something?"

"Hi, Alex," I said.

"Oh … hi, Emmeline," said Alex, recognizing me.

"Professor Prather!" exclaimed one of the officers. I instantly knew her as Sophie Barnes, one of my best literature students a year ago. In fact, she had changed her major to English for a short time—before her dad got word of it and said he wouldn't pay a penny more if she continued. Needless to say, she changed her major back to criminal justice and graduated on time.

"Sophie!" I said, giving her a hug. "As much as I think you would have made an excellent English teacher, I have to say I'm glad you're working for Copper Bluff's finest," I said. "I can see you're doing well."

"It's great. This is my first big case," Sophie said, unable to hide a small smile.

"I'm happy for you," I said. "I just wish the circumstances had been different."

"I know. I can't believe someone died in here." She looked around from floor to ceiling as if a ghost might appear any moment.

Sophie had always been a bit theatrical, so I wished I could think of a way to move her along now and catch up with her in private later. Her fellow officer, who judging from his gray hair and weathered skin was much older and presumably more experienced, was way ahead of me.

"Sophie forgot to introduce me. I'm Detective Beamer. And you are …?" he asked.

"I'm Emmeline Prather, and this is Lenny Jenkins. We both teach for the English Department."

"Emmeline Prather. You were one of Austin's teachers," he said.

"Yes, I was. I taught his English class, and I must say—"

He held up his hand. "I'll get to you later, Ms. Prather. Right now, we're interviewing personnel in the theater."

"Oh. Of course," I said. "Anytime."

Sophie quickly followed Detective Beamer's professional lead. "Well, we've got to get going. Maybe I'll see you around later. We'll be on campus all day."

"Yes. We will catch up soon. Goodbye," I said.

Alex, Lenny, and I watched them open the door and walk up the steps, a loud thud sounding behind them.

When they had gone, Alex shook his head. "Cops. I can't

believe I have to deal with them now on top of everything else."

"What happened this weekend?" I asked.

"I wish to hell I knew," said Alex. "One moment, we're ahead of schedule, and the next, a student dies on the set. Why the hell couldn't he have died *off* campus?"

"He was a student of mine," I said. "The one Dan spoke of in the meeting."

"Oh. Well, I'm very sorry for him, of course, but he's turned my theater upside down," said Alex.

"Did you know Austin?" asked Lenny. He had found a closed container and was sitting atop it, swinging his feet.

"No, no I didn't. I had seen him around … spoke to him a few times. A nice big kid like that … I was glad to have him on the set. I could see he'd make himself useful."

"So what happened?" I said.

"He was here this weekend. Several kids were, making costumes, practicing parts, putting together the set. That's what he would have been working on. Dan had an old white table that he wanted stripped of paint. It's perfect, just the wrong color for the Bishop's house. Next thing I know, the boy is found dead. That was Sunday."

"Who found him?" I asked.

"What'd he use to strip the paint?" asked Lenny at the same time.

Alex looked from me to Lenny. "You're from English, too, aren't you?"

"Yeah," said Lenny.

He nodded. "Well, I'm sure he used paint stripper. It's nothing unusual—it's what we always use. It couldn't have killed him, if that's what you're thinking. I told the police the same thing. We have plenty of toxins that could have. That just isn't one of them."

I wanted to ask where those toxins were kept, but I could sense that he was getting annoyed. We could still talk to Dan, so I repeated my initial question. "And who found him, did you say?"

He replaced a lid on one of the open containers and then stared at the one Lenny was sitting on. "No mystery there, either. The janitor."

I moved toward the door, motioning for Lenny to do the same. "Well, the cops will be out of your hair soon enough. Say, is Dan up in the theater? He's the one we were actually looking for."

"I'm sure he is—although he's done next to nothing all morning. He's pretty shook up about this whole thing. I hope that wears off soon."

"Death has a tendency to do that," said Lenny. "It always shakes me the hell up, anyway."

Alex stared at Lenny for a moment. "See you Friday, Emmeline."

"Right. I suppose you'll still want the committee to meet."

"Now more than ever," said Alex.

"Yes, good thinking. I'll see you then."

Lenny and I walked up the stairs in silence. I, at least, was all too aware of the eerie echo. When we reached the main hallway, I let the door shut softly behind me.

"He's the guy on that committee?" asked Lenny.

"One of them."

"Fun. Seems like a real control freak," said Lenny.

"I think so, too," I said, "but I don't really know him except from the group. He is nice enough, just bossy."

"Nice and bossy," said Lenny, opening the main theater door. "Not two attributes I look for in a group setting."

Dan was on the stage, just coming down from a ladder. It was propped up next to a false city wall still in need of paint. He didn't appear to have heard us come in.

When he reached the floor, I called out to him. "Dan!"

The theater lights glared down upon him, and he squinted and covered his brow with his hand. "Hello?"

"It's Emmeline," I said.

"And Lenny," whispered Lenny.

When we got closer, I said, "And you know Lenny Jenkins. He teaches English, too." I said it as if giving some sort of explanation for our presence.

Dan hung his legs over the stage and then jumped down. He brushed the hair from his eyes a few times and reached for Lenny's hand. "Hey, Lenny. Long time no see. Hi, Emmeline. Can you believe all this?"

I shook my head. "No, I can't. I imagine any moment I will awake and chide myself for reading too many mystery novels."

"I just …. Austin Oliver was a healthy kid, you know? Strong, too. How could he be dead? Alex tells me not to dwell on it, but I can't help but think something went very wrong down here."

Dan brushed his hair from his forehead again, and for the first time, I noticed his eyes were a nice shade of hazel. They were wide and framed with perfect feathery brows.

"Did you get to know him at all? Was there anything you discussed besides theater?" I asked.

"Not really." He thought for a moment. "He talked about science; I think that was where his real interests lay." He sat down in an aisle chair and motioned for us to sit as well. I sat in the chair across the aisle from him, and Lenny leaned up against the stage.

"It's surprising to me he would volunteer for the theater at all," I said.

Dan shook his head. "I don't think I ever saw him before the day he found me in the costume shop."

"Did he say why he wanted to work here? It's not like he got paid," asked Lenny.

Dan gave the question some thought. Finally he said, "You know, he really didn't. He was adamant about signing up, though. I asked him if he had ever worked in a theater before—you know, in high school or something—and he said no but he could do anything, said he was really good with his hands. I asked if he was interested in acting or anything like that, but he just laughed and said he wasn't into that. At the time I thought his reply was sort of odd. Usually we have the same group of kids hanging around. In some way, they all want to be … discovered. He wasn't here for that."

"It was probably about a girl," said Lenny. "She got him into it."

"For god's sake, Lenny," I exclaimed. "It's not always about a girl."

"Well, it's not *that* crazy of an idea," said Dan. "I did see him with a girl a few times. Sarah Sorenson—you know her? She was Fiona in *Brigadoon* last fall. A terrific singer."

"Yes, I do. Jane said she's a creative writer," I said.

"Ah. It makes sense now," said Lenny. "I told Em, when you're thinking about guys, you have to think about the girls they're dating … or want to date."

"Hold on. I said I'd seen him with her a few times, but I don't think they were dating. In fact, I'm pretty sure she's seeing another guy—dark hair, Asian maybe," said Dan. "He was around a lot last fall during rehearsal."

"Like I said, 'or want to date.' Maybe he was trying to steal her away from him."

Dan laughed softly. "I suppose he could have been. I don't know about any of that."

No one spoke for a long moment. Dan stared off into some unseen place, and Lenny looked around as if he had never been in a theater before.

"Dan, how do you think Austin died?" I asked.

Dan continued staring off but shook his head, so I knew he had heard me. Lenny looked at me and shrugged his shoulders.

"I think something happened, but I don't know what. You know what I mean?" Now he looked at me. "What I mean is I don't think he just 'died.' "

I nodded slowly. "Alex said something about paint remover. That Austin was refinishing a table. Do you think something could have happened there?"

"I don't think so. We use it all the time and in well-ventilated areas. Besides, Austin wore gloves. And I know he was wearing them the night he died because they're missing."

I raised my eyebrows.

He explained himself more carefully. "We have only one pair of industrial gloves that are a size extra large. Most kids wear medium or large at most. He must have been wearing them when they found him because the gloves are gone."

Lenny stood up straight, clearly interested. "Where do you keep that sort of stuff—paint removers, chemicals, gloves?"

"In the costume shop. There's a little cupboard in back."

"Is it locked?" I asked.

"Not the cupboard," Dan said. "But the costume shop is always locked. You have to know the pushbutton code to get in."

"Do a lot of people know the code?" asked Lenny.

"No, just us in the theater."

"Students, too, or just teachers?" Lenny continued.

Dan rubbed his palms on his faded jeans. Lenny's cannon-fire questions were starting to make him nervous.

"Both, I guess," he answered. "Alex and I and Martha—she's in the Art Department—plus about a dozen students. Maybe not quite that many."

His calm demeanor was beginning to crumble, and I felt we'd better leave soon before we induced a panic attack. "How long has it been since you've changed that code? Last semester?"

Dan shook his head but did not speak. I went over and stood next to Lenny.

"Never," he finally said. "I've never changed the code." His smile was rueful. "I never thought to."

Chapter Nine

—

DAN FOX SAID that Austin must have been wearing gloves the night of his death because they were missing from the theater. He assumed, and so did I, that the gloves were taken with the body. But what if, in fact, the gloves weren't with Austin? What if their disappearance were a clue to his death? The first thing we needed to ascertain was whether the gloves had ended up in the morgue with the body, and that we could do with a quick phone call to the coroner's office.

"Oh, so you want me to do your dirty work," Lenny said when I asked him to make the call.

We were crossing the street—he'd left his car at the theater—and his breath came quickly as we scurried along. Students were disappearing into classroom buildings now, but a few remained outside the student center, smoking cigarettes or eating sandwiches in wrappers from the Express, a convenience stop that carried mostly pre-packaged goods but also sliced pound cake with lemon icing that melted in your mouth. Whenever I had a need to go to the student center, usually to visit the bookstore, I couldn't resist buying at least one piece, carefully wrapped in cellophane.

Lenny was still frowning, and it puzzled me. He was never bad-tempered. "You're a bit cross."

"Sorry, I didn't get breakfast. I'm a maniac without food."

"I'll buy you lunch after this, I promise," I said.

"At Harry's," he said decidedly.

"Okay, at Harry's." Harry's was actually the Main Street Grill, but everyone called it Harry's because it was run by a little old man named Harry who liked to sip whiskey while he tended bar. He never appeared drunk, however, just easy-going and helpful. No matter what anyone asked, he would have a useful answer or story. The Main Street Grill also offered onion rings good enough to make it semi-famous. Unfortunately, the place was also famous for its pervasive odor of spilt beer, and the tables were always sticky with soda and rum. The food was sometimes worth the residue—the gossip, always. Harry himself made sure of this. He had an endless supply of news that in the course of an hour would pass from the bar to the surrounding booths and tables. He didn't make a big deal of it, just passed tidbits along as if it were his duty.

"Why do you want *me* to call, anyway?" asked Lenny.

I pretended to readjust my scarf to take his attention off what I was about to propose. "I thought you could say you are Dan Fox, from the theater, looking for your lost gloves. Of course you have to do it from the main office so it can't be traced by Caller ID back to us."

"Emmeline!" he said sternly, stopping in his tracks.

Several students looked in our direction, surprised that teachers could have anything going on in their own lives worth raising their voices about.

"Are you crazy?" he continued. "I'm pretty sure they call that … something I could be arrested for."

I grabbed his arm and resumed walking. "Keep your voice down. It's called 'interfering with an investigation,' and you won't be. It's just Dan Fox calling about his gloves; that's all."

"Unless they find out I'm not Dan Fox. Then it's called 'Lenny Jenkins is out of a job.' "

"Oh, don't be so dramatic," I said. "It's not as if we don't have good intentions. When we find out what really happened, you'll be a local hero. They might even name a classroom after you."

"Yeah, Jenkins's Jail Cell," Lenny mumbled. "This is what happens, kids, when you interfere with an official police investigation."

"Maybe they'll locate it in the Criminal Justice Department."

Lenny finally smiled. "Cute."

"Hey ... there's André. He's coming this way," I said, trying to keep my voice even. André was walking briskly toward us in a charcoal coat and matching hat, his maroon scarf whipping furiously in the wind. He saw us and waved.

"Oh, come on," said Lenny. "What is that, a beret?"

"Shhh," I hissed, waving and smiling.

"Maybe he could make the call. 'Yez, thiz eez Dan Fox. I am a looking for zee gloves. You have seen them, no?'"

"Good god, you sound like Count Dracula," I said under my breath. André was only a few steps away now.

"Bwahahah!" Lenny said, doing his best to imitate Count Dracula's laugh.

"Emmeline, Lenny, good afternoon." André shook both our hands vigorously. "It is cool out today."

"A bit breezy," I said, wishing I wouldn't have fooled around with my scarf. It had formed a fairly large knot right at my throat that I was sure looked less than chic.

"Ah. The wind. One gets used to it here," said André.

"It's as sure as death and taxes," added Lenny.

"Where are you on your way to?" asked André.

"We are on our way to make a very important—and very illegal—phone call," said Lenny. "How about you?"

André looked at me, and I rolled my eyes, dismissing the comment completely.

"I am going to the copy shop. I, too, am in the midst of something illegal." He winked at Lenny. "The grant office wants evidence of our French Department? I will give them evidence."

"Come on, André. You know Ms. Prather over here is banking on Paris. You're not going to disappoint her, are you?"

"I'm banking on no such thing," I said, but I doubted André could hear me over his own protests.

"Oh no, no. I will not screw up the thing. I will *fix* the thing," André said. Then he turned to me and smiled. "You shall see Paris ... or bust." He laughed at his own joke.

I didn't know what to say and felt myself turning pink. Hopefully the brisk wind had reddened my cheeks already. "Well, thank you. That would be nice."

"Come on, Em," said Lenny. "We can't stand here blushing all day. We have laws to break. See you around, André."

"Yes, I must go too," he said. "*Bonne chance, mes amis.*"

"You, too, André," I said. "Let me know how it goes." This I practically called out over my shoulder as Lenny was already walking briskly toward Harriman Hall.

Harriman Hall was quiet, as usual, for there were no real classrooms in the building except the few scattered in the basement. Most of the building was office space, where professors worked silently on papers or quizzes.

Lenny and I walked up the back steps to the second floor. Jane Lemort met us halfway up the stairs, looking vaguely gothic in her black dress, black tights, and long string of black pearls. She continued walking past us and then stopped. I knew with the skid of her big toe that she thought she had something clever to say; of course she never did.

"You two are unusually serious today. Why so quiet?" she asked with a dramatic question mark hanging over the end of her sentence.

Lenny smiled a little too widely. "We could tell you, Jane, but then we'd have to kill you."

She laughed in a high, lilting way. "Oh dear. One must keep one's secrets then."

Lenny kept walking, dismissing her completely. He turned left at the top of the stairs, toward his office. As he opened the door, an odor of pickle and onion wafted out.

"Why can't we talk in my office?" I asked, plugging my nose.

"We'd have to sit side by side," answered Lenny.

"And why doesn't the janitor empty your garbage?" I asked, motioning toward the overflowing Dodger's wastebasket in the corner.

"It's an un-standard trash receptacle. He's trying to force me to comply, but I refuse."

"That will teach him," I said.

"So what do I look up here? C for coroner?" asked Lenny.

"Use the Internet. Google it. It will be much faster."

He turned to his keyboard and typed in *coroner* and *Copper Bluff*.

"Hey, what do you know? There it is," he said. He wrote the phone number down on a piece of paper.

"What are you going to say? Do you want to … practice on me?"

"What? Do you mean like an accent?" he asked.

I was a bit nervous. They would figure it was a college student pulling a prank if Lenny called up using his unconvincing Irish brogue. "Not an accent, exactly. You're just going to try to sound like Dan Fox, right?"

He unzipped his coat. "Right. How does he sound?"

I gave this some thought. "He talks a bit more quietly than you do. His voice is softer, not quite so deep."

"Right, let's go."

We moved into the main office, after determining that Barb was on a break. Lenny had become adept at determining her break times, in order to avoid her, and this was one of them.

"Oh christ, Em. What are we doing? I can't do this. What if Barb or someone walks in?"

I dismissed his concern with a wave of my hand, trying to appear more confident than I truly was. "You'll be fine. It's one question: do they have the gloves? I'll watch at the door."

He nodded slowly as if trying to convince himself.

"I'm going to go now," I said.

He nodded again, and I left the office.

Outside Barb's door was a long rectangular table stacked with old books nobody wanted. There was an eclectic mix of textbooks, handbooks, novels—mostly written by retired professors—poetry collections, and pamphlets discussing the myriad causes one might support. I skimmed the assortment, trying to focus on some of the titles, but it was no use. My straining ears must have put my eyes out of focus because all I could see was the blur of black on white pages.

I heard a noise down the hall and noticed Giles walking in my direction. I tried to appear engrossed in a pamphlet on saving the white owls until he stood directly behind me.

"I didn't know you went for that environmental propaganda," he said, repeating the same language I had used last year at the Christmas party.

I tucked the pamphlet into my coat pocket. "Who isn't concerned about white owls? I certainly am. I've been a big fan ever since the Harry Potter series came out."

He smiled. "And how did your class go? Did your students have questions about Austin?"

"They did, but I didn't have any answers. I told them about the student services available on campus—typical administrative blabber."

Giles fastened the dark leather button on his corduroy jacket, and I found myself admiring his casual ways. I had seen him take close to a minute to retie one of his boots once while an entire class of students waited on an answer to a question.

"Very appropriate. Some of them might have been close to Austin."

I rolled my eyes. "Like the clowns in the back row? One of them called him a 'pussy' for volunteering in the theater. You'd think it were the 1950s, wouldn't you?"

"The 1950s—the dark ages," he sighed. "They're one in the same to you youngsters."

I smiled. I didn't think being twenty-eight made me a youngster, exactly. "No offense."

"None taken."

We stood in awkward silence, now that I had put away my pamphlet and he had finished asking his questions. He looked in Barb's office and then back at me. "Are you waiting for Barb?"

"Yes," I said, "though I'm not sure she's in there."

He motioned for me to go first.

"I just have a question about …."

He raised his eyebrows.

"The coffee fund." I could think of nothing I wanted to talk to her about less, but it was the first thing that came to mind.

He looked again at Barb's door. "Is someone else in there?"

"Hmm?" I pulled at my scarf. "Yes, Lenny," I said just as the office door opened.

"Em! He doesn't … oh, hi, Giles. What's up?" Lenny was flushed to the tips of his ears.

Giles crossed his arms. "Hello, Lenny. What's *up* with you?"

"I was looking for Barb," Lenny said. "She always wants to know Harry's pie of the day. But he doesn't have pecan today. And on the cusp of fall. Can you believe it? Em's buying me lunch. Do you want to come?"

Despite his lie, Lenny sounded quite convincing, and I had a feeling he could go on like this for several minutes if he had to.

"No thank you. I try to avoid that gossip mill around lunch hour. It breeds indolence."

Lenny looked at me.

"Laziness," I said.

Giles shook his head and walked into Barb's office.

Lenny quickly pulled his own door shut and led me several steps down the stairs before saying another word. "They don't have them. The gloves. They don't have them."

"Do you know what this means?" I whispered.

"Of course I do."

But I couldn't resist saying it anyway. "We find the gloves, and we find the evidence that someone else was involved in Austin's death—someone with something to hide."

Chapter Ten

———

HARRY'S WAS ALWAYS packed this time of day, and today was no exception. The pub thrummed with life, its clientele ranging from old men in woolen caps to college kids in stocking caps. Only in a college town could you go into a grill on a weekday afternoon and witness men and boys alike drinking beer and eating peanuts—carefree, content, happy.

The talk was as wonderfully diverse as the clothing. The farmer on the corner stool talked about soybean prices and the a.m. radio show while the boy in the next booth discussed Milton and his captivating portrayal of the devil in *Paradise Lost*. I felt myself cocooned in this blithe world when I came, unable to take much of anything seriously, and I suppose that was the source of Giles's caution. But this afternoon, sitting across from a friend in a tall, sticky booth, I felt nothing could drive me away—even the threat of indolence.

Lenny took a swig from his frosty mug, the foam gathering at his lips. "That's better."

I sipped my beer carefully to avoid the foam.

We sat for a while in silence, listening to the broken conversation of others. Once in a while we would smile at each other, hearing some student's account of an awful class, an unfair test, or a boring teacher. Then Lisa, a large woman with an even larger chest, brought out our steaming hot onion rings, setting the plate down with a loud thump, and we were both startled out of our congenial quiet.

Lenny untangled one of the onion rings from the top of the pile and held it close to his mouth. "Do you think we're really onto something? With the gloves, I mean."

I set down my beer, nodding. "Yes, I believe we are."

"So what are we going to do about it?" He bit into the onion ring, which was probably still too hot. His quick reach for the beer confirmed my suspicions.

"We're going to find the gloves," I said simply.

His dark eyebrows were intense anyway because they were such a contrast to his light hair; now that they were furrowed, they gave him a portentous air. "But don't you see? We're talking about *murder.*"

This word he said so quietly I could barely hear it. "Well of course," I said, grabbing an onion ring. "That is the word for intentionally causing a death."

He continued, "I'm serious. Murderers don't just walk into a small town like Copper Bluff and start killing students. For what reason?"

"People kill people for all sorts of reasons—and not just in big cities. Maybe Austin made someone angry, or he threatened someone, or maybe he wasn't the one who was supposed to die. Maybe it was Alex. He can be quite condescending. Look at Jane Lemort. Don't tell me she doesn't have it coming."

He put down his beer. "I can see you've put some thought into this."

I munched on another onion ring. "I couldn't sleep last night. I ran several different scenarios in my head."

"Hey," he said, taking the biggest onion ring for himself, "I'm just saying that if we're really talking about murder then we'd better be careful—and not just for the reasons Giles mentioned. If Austin was murdered, then we have a murderer living in town, maybe on campus. He might be willing to do it again if we start poking around."

"Or *she*. It could be a she," I said.

Now he was positively glowering.

I took a sip of my beer and leaned back in the booth. "You know, I like this for a change—you being the serious one, all tangled up in knots."

"Well I don't. It makes me feel responsible. I didn't even know the damn kid and now you ...."

I raised my eyebrows.

"You're too damn charming. You ... you've charmed me into it." He grabbed another large onion ring.

"I want to take that as a compliment, but you're making it very difficult with that sour look on your face," I said.

He, too, leaned back. "Let's just take it slow, okay? You have a tendency to ... *rush* to conclusions."

"I do not!" I said hotly.

Now he smiled.

"Well, sometimes I do, but those conclusions are usually right."

Now he raised one eyebrow, a skill I'd never been able to master.

I stood my ground. "Seventy-five percent of the time at least."

The waitress interrupted with two Reuben sandwiches, piled high with corned beef and sauerkraut, and crinkly French fries that were just as hot and tasty as the onion rings. Our conversation turned to insignificant things—old houses, old songs, old poets, and old games—from baseball to mahjong. We were too young for all this, but our pasts were somehow steeped with it, maybe from old books, maybe from this old town. It didn't really matter, because we both understood, and neither one of us had to explain.

A couple of the old men were shaking their heads and laughing as they talked to Harry, who was wiping glasses and hanging them above the bar. By contrast, Harry's face was rather serious and set. I stopped listening to Lenny for a moment so I could catch what was being said.

"There ain't been nothing like that in these parts ever, Harry," said the laughing man. He wore a red and white cap and under his overalls a red shirt, stretched tightly over his large belly.

The other man, scrawny and wrinkled, said, "No, sir. Nothing like that in Copper Bluff."

Harry was getting irritated. You could tell by the way he began to wipe the glasses more vigorously. "Well, I know what I know."

The man in the red and white cap slapped his knee and laughed again. "That ain't much!"

"I know a boy doesn't just up and die for no reason, and I know a cop doesn't come around asking questions for no reason, and I know when you, Jerry, have had too much to drink. You'd best be getting home to Alma before I call her myself."

At this, the old man pulled down the ear flaps on his cap, reached into his middle pocket, and threw a ten-dollar bill on the counter. He was no longer laughing.

"See you tomorrow, Jerry," said the thin one. Jerry grunted a reply and left.

Harry took a drink from his glass of whiskey, wiping underneath it with his bar rag. "Amateur."

The thin man kept his head down, content not to respond.

I turned my attention back to Lenny, who from the look of his face had also eavesdropped on the conversation. He finished the last of his beer, placing the heavy mug back on the napkin with a thud. "It looks like we're not the only ones with suspicions."

I finished my beer also. "And Giles thinks we read too much Poe."

Chapter Eleven

—

THE NEXT DAY, I arrived on campus bright and early. Though I didn't teach on Tuesdays, I knew Lenny did, and I wanted to talk with him about what I'd mentally dubbed "The Case." Dan had mentioned two things of interest: the gloves, which we had discussed at some length at Harry's, and Sarah Sorenson. I didn't know Sarah personally, but I was certain I could find someone in the English Department who did. I needed to know if she was the girl from the parking lot—if she was the one who had threatened Austin.

As I entered Lenny's office, I braced for an odor, but surprisingly, there was very little. He must have eaten at home—or at least thrown the food wrappers into another receptacle. When he noticed me eyeballing the trashcan, he explained, "Barb. I've been sneaking it into her office."

I furrowed my brow. "Are you sure you really want to get on her bad side?"

"I didn't know she had a good side," he said as he laid down his pen. He had been making notes in a spiral notebook, probably his day's lesson plan, when I came in. Now that he'd put down his pen, I hoped he had enough material to keep his students busy for at least an hour and fifteen minutes.

"So let me guess what brings you to campus on a Tuesday," he said. "Austin."

"Yes and no. I was thinking over what Dan said about Sarah. And that night in the parking lot. I kept wondering if Sarah might be the girl Austin was arguing with. Do you know her?"

He shook his head. "Not personally, but she'll be easy enough to get ahold of. I mean, she's right here in our department. Who's got her? Giles? Probably Dunsbar, if she's a creative writer."

I nodded. "I think so. Giles would know, and so would Barb. But you heard Giles: I'm in a fragile state. We can't risk him knowing about our inquiries."

"Right. I agree."

I stared at him blankly for a moment. "We agree? Oh dear. I'm in a more fragile state than Giles realizes."

Lenny leaned back in his chair. "I think I like this new fragile state. It's a hell of a lot more exciting than … what's an antonym for 'fragile'?"

"Indestructible?"

Lenny shrugged. "Not exactly what I was looking for but yeah, whatever."

I laughed.

Someone knocked at the door.

"Come in," Lenny said.

It was Claudia Swift. We both breathed sighs of relief.

"Oh, I had a feeling I'd find you here," said Claudia. She found a folding chair beside his bookshelf and unfolded it. Sitting down, she carefully spread out her full broom skirt around her chair. "It's hardly believable, is it? One of our students, dead."

"Did you know him, too?" I asked.

"Well, I didn't have him in any of my classes, exactly, but I still considered him every bit one of my own students," said Claudia.

"Of course," said Lenny.

"I'm going to have my creative writing students write eulogies today and select the best ones to read at his memorial service, a week from today, " said Claudia.

"You're a creative writer!" I exclaimed as if I hadn't taught alongside her for a year. Maybe she had Sarah in one of her classes.

She didn't notice. "Certainly I am, but I think the *students* should have the opportunity to memorialize their fellow student, don't you?"

I quickly recovered. "Yes, you're right. Do you have many students in that class?"

She seemed to be recalling each student's face as she counted. "Oh I suppose ... twenty or so."

"Twenty. That's quite a few for a creative writing class," I said. "Do you know Sarah—"

"Sorenson," Lenny added.

"Sarah, yes. Of course. She's a poet ... and a pretty good one." She looked between Lenny and me. "Why do you ask?"

"I think she was a friend of Austin's. Maybe even a *good* friend," I said, hoping she'd catch my drift.

"Really? I don't think so. I'm pretty sure she dates Sean Chan," said Claudia.

"Sean Chan?" asked Lenny. "How do you know that?"

I, too, was rather surprised that she would be able to recall a first and last name for the boyfriend of one of her students but said nothing.

She walked over to his coffee pot and examined a chipped cup. "May I?"

"Sure," said Lenny. "It's a couple hours old though."

She poured a cup anyway.

She sat back down and crossed her legs, perching the cup atop her knee. "When you teach creative writing, you get to know your students ... intimately. They write about their mothers, fathers, boyfriends, girlfriends, companions, cats, dogs, family vacation spots. No topic is barred. We allow our creative energy to reign supreme—"

"So she writes about him in her poems?" Lenny broke in.

I was glad of his question, for once Claudia got on the topic of creative energy, it was hard to get her off.

"Yes. That, and I met him once at the spring banquet, when Sarah was awarded a Binger Scholarship." She went to take a sip of her coffee and then stopped. Perhaps she had seen something floating in the cup. She set down the cup and looked at Lenny. "You are acting peculiar today. Don't think I haven't noticed."

Lenny gave her his usual warm, boyish smile. "What about Em? Is she acting peculiar?"

"Em is always peculiar … in a good, quirky way," she added when she noticed my frown. "You, however, are a constant. Except for today."

I laughed at this and so did Lenny. Claudia, though, remained quite serious.

I stretched out my legs and tried to appear casual. If I knew Claudia, she would not want me distressing one of her students or disturbing her creative energy. "So, what time is class?"

She looked at her watch. "In about fifteen minutes. I'd better get going."

"Which way?" I said, standing up. "I'll walk with you."

"Oh, it's right here, downstairs. It couldn't be a worse location. But I have to stop at my office."

Lenny and I watched Claudia leave. "I have to get going," I said after she left.

"Tell me what Sarah says, okay?" he said in a low voice.

"I will," I said and walked out of his office and down the stairwell.

Harriman Hall had very few classrooms in the basement— five at the most—so it was no trouble finding Claudia's. Two of the classrooms were completely dark. In one was a male professor writing on the blackboard, and in another, a teaching assistant already sitting in the corner, taking attendance. Claudia had to be teaching in the room in the farmost corner with the four small windows.

I knew what Sarah looked like, vaguely, so when I peered into the classroom and did not see her long, dark hair, I knew she had not yet arrived. Several minutes remained before class, and I hoped she might arrive early. I was not disappointed. Within a few minutes, I saw a dark-haired girl with a small quilted knapsack coming down the stairs. She was tall and slender, with pale, fine-pored skin and willowy arms. I couldn't imagine this waifish girl threatening Austin. Still, I was determined to ask her a few questions. As she approached me, she raised her eyes.

"You're Sarah, right?" I said.

She nodded but said nothing.

"I'm Emmeline Prather. I teach in the English Department."

She nodded again. "Is Professor Swift sick today?"

"No, nothing like that. I just wanted to talk with you for a few moments about a student of mine. Austin? Austin Oliver?" I walked a few steps down the hall. "Could you join me for a few minutes?"

Sarah looked at the classroom and then back at me. "Sure."

We were several feet away from the classroom before I began to speak. "I'm sure you know Austin was found dead on Sunday."

She nodded. "Yes, I know, but I still can't believe it."

She stopped near the restroom, and I supposed this was as far as she was willing to go. I'd have to talk quickly. "How did you know Austin?" I asked.

"I knew him from theater. He was working on the set. I'm playing Fantine."

Her voice had a lilt to it that could have conveyed anything, and I could see why she was popular in the theater crowd. It was possible she was doing a nice bit of acting right now. Still, I couldn't match her voice with the one from the parking lot.

"Oh, how wonderful! You did an excellent job in *Brigadoon*," I said, playing up to her vanity. "Had you known Austin a long time, then?"

She shook her head. "No, not really. Just since the beginning of the school year. But he was so *nice*, so different from the other guys on campus. I liked him."

She seemed genuinely upset, and I began to feel uncomfortable. I didn't want to add to her grief if she were truly close with Austin. "Were you dating, then?"

"No," she answered a little too quickly. "Who told you that?"

"No one," I replied. "You said you liked him, so I just assumed—"

"Oh. No, I didn't mean it like that. I meant I liked the way he was, you know, so different ... so considerate. He didn't have to shove his ego in your face every ten seconds to make himself feel important. Plus, he was helping with the play. My boyfriend doesn't even know who Fantine is."

I sympathized with her. "He must not be in theater then."

She shook her head. "Nope. Chemistry."

"So yours was a ... platonic friendship with Austin."

"*Completely.*"

I nodded, but that didn't mean I believed her. "Did he ever mention any problems he had with family or school or friends?

"No. He was trying to get into that fraternity, although I don't know why. They're a bunch of jerks, not Austin's style at all."

"I was surprised by that too. I was also surprised he was working in the theater. He wasn't a fan of literature in my class."

She looked back at her classroom. "I think he enjoyed working with his hands. He grew up on a farm, you know."

"Yes, I know. One more question, and I'll let you get back to class," I said in an even voice. "When was the last time you saw Austin?"

She continued to look past me. "Thursday, I think."

I waited for more, and I was not disappointed. It was surprising how many times not saying anything at all would prompt others to continue talking.

"I was supposed to meet up with him on Saturday, but I didn't. I didn't meet him."

I looked at her directly. "Where were you to meet?"

She stared at me for a moment, as if she didn't want to say, and then said, "The theater."

"What time was this supposed to happen?" My questions were coming out more quickly than I intended, but I, too, was in a rush to get out of there before Claudia arrived.

"That night, around seven, but like I said, I couldn't make it. I ended up working late. Professor Prather, I'd really better get back …."

I began walking with her down the hall. "Of course," I said. "Thank you for your help."

"Oh sure. It was nothing," she said, continuing toward her classroom.

I paused at the stairwell. "Oh, by the way, did you enjoy yourself at the poetry slam?"

She looked back. "Yeah, it was fun," she said. "I had a good time."

"Next time maybe I'll get a chance to hear some of your work."

She smiled. "You'll have to ask Professor Swift."

As I continued up the stairs, I became certain of one thing: Sarah had been with Austin the night of the poetry reading, which meant Lenny was right. They'd probably been seeing each other in some capacity. After all, Austin had befriended her with vigor and even attended an event that I had to presume did not interest him at all. In fact, she could have been the reason for his volunteering at the theater. It certainly was a plausible explanation. Still, both Dan Fox and Sarah had said she and Austin met *while* working at the theater, so that explanation didn't exactly pass the litmus test.

I stopped at the vending machine on the main entrance floor. I had a sweet tooth, a weakness widely known in my circle. Anytime anybody wanted something of me, they usually approached me with a Kit Kat or some other piece of chocolate. The ploy was often effective.

I pushed E5 and waited for the telltale plunk. Meanwhile, I noticed the wire rack by the door overflowing with a special edition of *Campus Views*, our student newspaper. On the front cover was a picture of Austin Oliver with the headline, "Student Found Dead in Campus Theater." I started scanning the article, then tucked it under my arm as I retrieved the candy bar and continued up the stairs toward my office.

I opened my window—the small room was stuffy and warm in the afternoon sun—and spread out the newspaper to the second and third pages. The article contained short interviews with Austin's professors—all except me. Apparently I could not be reached for comment. For a moment, I was incensed. I had never been contacted for an interview. Nobody had asked me my opinion. Then I looked up at my desk phone and saw that the red light was blinking. I rummaged through my purse; my cellphone had inadvertently been left on Do Not Disturb, and I had three new voicemails. I shook my head. I really needed to keep better track of my phones.

I was able to determine Austin's fall schedule from the list of professors in the article; there were three of them, besides me, who had better insight into Austin's character than the rest of the college. This would be extremely helpful in determining his actions during his last days on campus. The first one was Owen Jorgenson, the science professor and Ann's husband. He taught freshmen earth science classes in a lecture-style hall, so his comments revealed very little beyond the fact that Austin was always attentive in class and participatory in lab, even staying late to help set up lab trays. The second was Martha Church, who taught art appreciation, which would have met the fine arts requirement Austin needed to graduate. Her comments were more flowery but no more revealing than Owen's. She talked of Austin's interest in set design and his involvement in this semester's play, for which she credited herself. The third, then, was Robert Reynolds, who was a military science instructor for ROTC. He stated that Austin was a fine young man who was making "swell" progress in his leadership and personal development class. He also said he knew Austin's family and that they could be proud of Austin's involvement in the program.

I pushed back my chair. Austin's composition class met Mondays, Wednesdays, and Fridays. Friday morning, Austin did not show up, but he was on campus because he came to my office. I wondered if any of his other classes met Friday and if he'd missed those as well. This would make me feel somewhat better about him missing my class; perhaps the poetry recitation had nothing at all to do with his absence.

The only way to know for certain was to ask his other professors if their classes met that day and if he'd been absent. If I remembered correctly, science courses usually met on Tuesdays and Thursdays with a lab component scheduled once a week. Professor Jorgenson's account would therefore not reveal much; the last day he saw Austin was probably Thursday, and I doubted his lab was scheduled on a Friday afternoon. If I knew little about science classes, I knew even less about military science courses, or ROTC, and was unsure how they were even prefixed. Students who continued the program in their junior and senior years had to enroll in the National Guard or Army Reserve upon completion of their program. For their enrollment, they received a reduction in their college debt.

Art appreciation, then, had the best chance of meeting on Friday, as it probably met on Mondays, Wednesdays, and Fridays—same as my class. I decided I would talk to Martha Church first, which gave me another reason to go back to the theater building. I was certain it held the answers I sought—if not the answers then at least the people who knew them.

I heard voices outside my door and realized one of them was Giles's. The other male voice was harder to identify, yet it sounded familiar. I folded the newspaper quietly and carefully as I tried to eavesdrop. I didn't have to listen long, however, because Giles was knocking on my door and asking to come in—a rare request.

"Come in," I said, hastily clearing my throat.

To my surprise, the police officer from the theater was standing next to Giles, who looked calm and perfectly at ease.

"Professor Prather, this is Officer Beamer," said Giles, stepping aside so that the officer could enter. "He has a few questions he'd like to ask you about Austin Oliver."

"Hello again," said Beamer.

"Again?" said Giles, slightly elevating the word into a question. He shook his head and pulled the door behind him. "Do assist him with anything he requires, Emmeline."

"Of course," I said. I motioned to the chair directly across from me. "Have a seat."

Beamer complied, looking around at the books on the shelves as he made himself comfortable. "You read all these?"

I nodded. "Pretty much."

He grunted. "I can't seem to get through any of the books my wife gives me. I must be doing something wrong."

"Maybe they're the wrong books," I said.

He seemed to like this idea. "Hmm. That's a thought."

"So how can I help you, Mr. Beamer?"

He pulled out a small notebook from an even smaller shirt pocket. A pencil stub was tucked inside the wire binding. "Well, we're gathering information about Mr. Oliver's last days here on campus. Pretty routine. I talked to the folks over at the theater, as you know, and I figured it wouldn't hurt to talk to some of his teachers, too. Now, you taught his English class … is that right?"

"That's correct," I said.

"Would you say he was a good student?"

"Yes, I would," I said. "He didn't necessarily *like* English, but he always showed up for class and completed his assignments on time."

He wrote something in his notebook. "So he didn't like your class."

"He didn't like *English*," I corrected him, hoping he would make a change in the notebook. He did not.

"Did he have any friends in the class?" Beamer asked.

I thought about this carefully. I didn't know if Austin would have considered Jared and Adam his friends, but they were certainly acquaintances. "He did sit next to two boys in the back row, Adam and Jared, whom he seemed to know in some capacity. I believe they belong to a fraternity Austin was trying to join."

Beamer nodded but wrote down nothing, so I felt compelled to keep going. "Austin didn't seem like the fraternity type to me, so one wonders why he would want to join."

"I think they're sort of popular, aren't they, fraternities?" said Beamer, stretching his legs. "If you can get into one, you're pretty neat. Maybe he wanted to be one of the cool kids."

I raised my eyebrows. "Maybe."

"But you don't think so. You think something else. You think he had ulterior motives."

I nodded vigorously. He was beginning to understand.

"But you don't know what those ulterior motives were."

"No, I don't."

He made another notation on his pad. "So did your class meet on Friday?"

I nodded.

"And how did Austin appear to you?"

I leaned forward. "He didn't show up."

He looked up from his notepad.

"But," I continued, "he *did* stop by my office Friday morning. And I must say that he seemed different ... worried, even."

Beamer furrowed his forehead, which had a deep crease from performing this action frequently. "What did you talk about?"

"A poem, mostly. Originally, I thought he had come to see me about a poem he was supposed to read for class."

"Maybe he was worried about reading the poem in front of everyone," said Beamer.

I shook my head. "I thought so at first, but now I think it was something else."

Beamer looked at me.

"He wasn't wearing his backpack," I said. "Maybe you should write that down: He wasn't wearing his backpack."

Beamer crossed his short arms as if to make a point that he would write down only what he saw fit to write down. "Ms. Prather, it's obvious to me that you believe something mysterious is at play here."

"And you don't?" I questioned, deciding not to tell him about the parking lot incident.

Now he uncrossed his arms and leaned forward a bit. He was much older than I'd thought, probably closer to sixty than fifty, with strong gray streaks of hair at his temples and sides.

"Here's the thing, Ms. Prather. When a person dies, people look back over the last few days of that person's life and find 'clues' foretelling the person's death. Now, I don't know if it's superstition or religion or just human nature that does it. All I know is that every case I've ever worked has had some of that. Even when the person dies from old age, relatives will say, 'Edna knew it was her last day. She ate all her favorite foods, remember?' That sort of talk. Maybe it just makes us feel better. I don't know. But what I do know is that it's foolish to start down a path that is bound to lead to nowhere."

"Can I ask you then what you think happened to Austin?" I said.

"Well, I don't know. That's what I'm trying to find out," he said with a short laugh.

"But you don't have any indications that he died under suspicious circumstances?"

Beamer grew serious. "I'll be straight with you. Nineteen-year-old kids don't just up and die for no reason. You know that, and I know that. Does that make me suspicious? You bet. Does that mean I'm worried the kid wasn't wearing his backpack on Friday? Probably not."

"But you should be," I protested. "If he wasn't on his way to English class, where was he on his way to—or from?"

His laughter this time was accompanied by a snort, yet I had a feeling he was taking me more seriously than he let on. He stood and tucked his notepad back into his pocket.

"You know, if he liked your class a bit more, Ms. Prather, maybe he would have shown up Friday. Maybe you should be worried about that."

I opened my mouth and then shut it. I could think of no rebuttal.

He touched the tip of his hat. "Have a nice day."

Chapter Twelve

—

THERE WAS A tree on campus I thought of as my friend. It was tall and bushy, and this time of year a scarlet red. It stood on the corner of Elm and Fifth Street, and every time I walked by it, I felt our connection as I silently recalled the events of my day, as if the tree had observed also and might reply in kind. It was the last of the trees to let go of its leaves, and I wanted to believe this was more or less for my benefit. Willa Cather had it right. Sparse as they were on the plains, trees became friends, or if not friends, then acquaintances and landmarks. They told one where to stop, where to turn, where to pass. I could navigate all of Copper Bluff—and a good portion of the surrounding countryside—by trees alone.

After my interview with Detective Beamer, going for a drive in the country was a lot less appealing than sitting in a cozy booth in a warm sweater, and eating at a nice restaurant would get me off campus and among people who did not know me as "teacher."

It had drizzled just enough to make the streets black and shiny, and as I walked under the yellow glow of the streetlamps, I imagined the town in watercolors, bleeding one into another until no buildings remained, only blobs of light. I pulled my wool peacoat tighter as the wind found me on Seventh Street, making short work of my flimsy scarf, and I ducked into Dynasty, a sophisticated restaurant that served authentic Cantonese cuisine. Mostly retired professors and elderly couples ate here, for the prices were considered outlandish in a town where students could visit the all-you-can-eat Chinese buffet for just $6.99 a plate. But on trying days such as this one, I told myself I could afford to splurge. I enjoyed the reserved atmosphere, the quiet hum of voices, and the padded footsteps of the waitresses. It was conducive to thought on a night such as this.

The hostess seated me in a booth and handed me a slim menu. I ordered the Cantonese wanton soup and hot tea, and within minutes, a tiny brown pot and handleless cup arrived. I drank eagerly, feeling the mild liquid warm my throat and chest, while admiring the muted pink walls and sparse paintings of birds. As I sat in the booth, time seemed suspended and the town itself ceased to exist. My mind could wander the whole wide world without ever leaving the restaurant.

When André walked in, I immediately noticed his look of consternation, and I selfishly prayed that nothing was the matter with him, too. I wanted him to be most of all carefree, for that was what France represented to me: leisurely strolls along the Seine, long lunches in outdoor cafés, unusual care devoted to the arrangement of beautiful scarves. I knew the overworked look of Americans too well and was dismayed to see it written on André's face. Once I called to him, though, his look changed to pleasure, and he pointed the hostess in my direction.

"Em! Good evening," he said.

"Hello, André. Join me, won't you?"

He sat opposite me, surveying the table. "You are finished, are you not? I do not want to keep you."

"I am," I said, "but I would enjoy the company. I've been sitting here too long by myself."

"I know women who would rather starve than eat by themselves," said André, turning over his menu.

"Thankfully, I'm not one of those women."

He raised his head and smiled. "No, of course not. And I'm glad for it."

I nodded toward the window. "It's beginning to rain again."

"I love the rain here. It never rains, and when it does, the sky falls."

"It does, doesn't it?" I said.

"In Paris, it drizzles." He put down his menu. "Everything there is temperate, even the rain."

"What is it like there, really?" I asked. He was always somewhat hesitant with his answers about his home country, and I could never quite figure out why.

"Paris is … what can I say? Some Frenchmen hate Paris. So do some Americans. There is a jealousy, I think. But the city is most beautiful if it is exhilaration—*joie de vivre*—that you seek."

"I think I would like it." This I said more to myself than to André, but he replied anyway.

"Em, you would never leave. I would take you back to the States kicking and shouting," he chuckled.

I smiled. He enjoying using colloquialisms, although they never came out quite right. "What about you?" I asked.

"*Mais non.* I was never a city boy. I come from an area much like this. I feel at home here."

"Me, too," I agreed. The waitress approached, and André ordered. When the waitress left, I said, "When you first walked in, you seemed distressed."

"I was. I am. They require more information for my grant to be approved," he said.

I refilled my teacup. "That's a good thing, isn't it? That means it hasn't been denied."

"Normally I would say yes, but the information they want I cannot give. We have no advanced French courses, not yet."

"Have you talked to Dean Richardson?"

André flung his hands in the air. "I talk to him, but he is a thick-headed man. All he wants to talk about is Spanish and German. German! Who speaks German besides the Germans?"

I had no answer for him, and furthermore, it was hard for me to concentrate on what he was saying with his hair swept across his forehead the way that it was, tussled from the wind.

"I will get this grant, Em. If I don't, I shall move to Canada. It cannot be much colder there than it is here."

I refocused immediately. "Oh no, we can't let you do that. You would abhor the accent. And besides, it *is* much colder. I had a student from Canada once. He said he slept in his coat."

A small smile crept across his face. "I think you tell stories."

"Not tell stories—just stretch the truth," I said.

A plate of steaming noodles appeared, smattered with fresh vegetables. "Ah," he said in appreciation. "This helps. Food always helps." He took several large bites. "So what brings you out on this cold night?"

I folded my napkin and placed it back on the table. "Oh, I don't know. I guess I just needed to be among the living. That student who died? He was in my class."

André put down his chopsticks. "It is a tragedy. I am so sorry. I read about it in the paper, and I said to myself, 'Something is not right here. Something has happened to this boy.'"

"Yes. That's exactly what I said. But everyone goes about their business as if it's all routine, as if this sort of thing happens all the time in Copper Bluff."

He picked up his sticks again and pointed them at me. "*Allez!* These routines only make them feel better. See, we are all in a masquerade. We stop to ask questions and now the play has stopped. Now we are not happy."

"Indeed," I said. "You are right. You see exactly what I mean."

"Of course. You and I are on the same book."

I smiled, noticing a small disturbance near the cash register out of the corner of my eye. Really, I had overheard pieces of it several times during our conversation but had not bothered to look over. A young Asian man, college-aged, was arguing with the hostess. They spoke in Chinese, but it had gone on for a long time. Although the young man seemed angry, visibly so, he also seemed to defer to the woman, who was older than he was. She tried to quiet him by briskly shaking her head. I turned my head suddenly at what I thought was the word "Sean" inserted in the conversation, although it could have been my imagination. He grabbed her wrist, which she immediately shook off. He had gone too far and was left staring after her. He spun around, stalking out of the restaurant.

When I turned back toward our table, André was watching the young man go. "What was that about? I bet you have already imagined a hundred possibilities."

"You're getting to know me too well."

"It is impossible to know someone too well. Besides, you are always a mystery to me. I see you watching those persons, and I say to myself, 'What is she thinking? She is always thinking.' Then I am not as interesting as I thought before I sat down."

I laughed. "How can you say that? You are the most interesting person I know."

"Or the most French. There is a difference."

I shrugged and took a drink of my water. He had a point. Much of my affection for André had to do with my affection for French culture. "Either way, I've got to get going. The rain has stopped now."

"You are in a hurry to follow that boy?"

I stood. "Of course not." I tucked my scarf into my coat. "Goodnight."

"Goodnight, Emmeline. Be careful. It is cold out there."

Indeed, if I still could have seen the boy, I would have followed him. He might have been Sean Chan. But the night was dark, and few people were out. I put my head down and walked into the wind, my cheeks stinging from the cold. The air smelled like autumn—fresh, but with a hint of wood smoke and the musky scent of wet leaves; the afternoons would no longer grow warm and muggy, but colder and darker. The season would become more serious as October approached and winter looked on like an eager zealot. But I did not mind. I was a person of change who constantly looked ahead, even if she did not like what she saw.

Chapter Thirteen

THE COLD SNAP continued into Wednesday, yet the heat had not yet been turned on in most of the campus buildings. The Fine Arts Building, though, was newer, so the cold didn't penetrate the walls as it did in Harriman Hall. I had been reduced to wearing fingerless gloves in my office.

After teaching my morning Composition 101 class, I decided to pay a visit to Martha Church. The Art Department, after all, was in close proximity to the theater. Maybe she knew Austin from his work on the set. She might have even encouraged him to volunteer. And I needed to find out if he had attended her class the Friday before his death.

I knocked lightly on the door.

"Come in!" she said.

I found Ms. Church in a square office with a large window, looking at students' pencil drawings, turning them every which way in the bright light of the window. She had frizzy blonde hair, shoulder-length and quite becoming, and long fingers, noticeably strong and agile.

She told me to sit down for a moment while she finished.

After scribbling something in her green-leather grade book, she shut it hastily. "How can I help you?"

"I'm Emmeline Prather. I teach in the English department—"

"Oh, I bet you know Ann Jorgenson."

"Yes," I said, excited that we had at least one thing in common.

"I adore Ann. She is such a pleasure to work with. She has been indispensible to this production and my costume design. There isn't a period of history that she doesn't know exactly what women were wearing."

"She is so bright," I agreed. "I tell her all the time she could have been an English professor. In fact, she does teach classes for our department."

She motioned to one of the chairs across from her desk. "Please."

"Thank you," I said, sitting down. "There's another person we both knew: Austin Oliver. We both had him in our classes."

She leaned back in her chair. "Oh, of course. I remember your name from the article. I knew I had heard it before! Can you imagine?"

I shook my head. "No, I can't. He never showed up for my class on Friday. I wonder, did he show up for yours?"

"Why no! He didn't. My class meets at nine o'clock, so I have a rigorous attendance policy. He came to every class except that one. I went back and checked," said Martha.

"And why did you do that?" I asked.

She straightened her back. "What? Go back and check his attendance record? I don't know …." She stared at the door for a long time and then shrugged. "I suppose I wanted to know if I had seen him the day before he … passed. That is sort of gruesome, isn't it?"

"Not at all," I said. "You probably thought it was odd that he didn't attend your class the day before he died, when he had attended all the others."

"Do you?" she asked, her eyes widening. "Do you think it was odd?"

I didn't see any reason to lie. "Yes, I do."

"Well!"

I glanced at the students' drawings scattered beneath her grade book. "Did Austin ever draw anything ... peculiar?"

"No. His was a class that studied art; they didn't *make* art. It's an introductory course, a fine arts credit. That's all. I'm sure he saw it as nothing else."

"Oh," I said.

"But he did doodle," she added hopefully. "As an art professor, I notice these things."

"Do you remember what he doodled?" I asked, leaning toward her desk.

She tapped her pen several times.

"A man. Yes, I think it was a man."

"Was it anyone you'd recognize?" I asked.

"Oh heavens no. If he had that sort of talent, I would have recruited him for my drawing classes. But as I said, he didn't care too much for art."

"And what about theater? Did he have a talent for that?"

"I think so. He was a hard worker and good at making things for the set. And you know? I think he really liked the play. He was always coming around asking questions about production. Of course, I told him I had nothing to do with the play itself. I only design the costumes."

It was hard to believe Austin inquired about any piece of literature, let alone a French musical based on a classic novel. From what I had seen, he completed my assignments only because he cared about his grade-point average. In fact, I had the feeling that he believed literature—and perhaps art as well—was a flat out waste of his time. I concluded Austin's reason for inquiring about the play had to do with one person—Sarah Sorenson.

I nodded and glanced at my watch. It was eleven thirty, and I was ravenous. "You've been so helpful."

"Have I? I don't know."

I smiled. "You have." Then I stood up.

"Emmeline?"

"Yes?"

"Did anything happen in your class that was … peculiar? Is that why you're here?"

"Peculiar? No, not at all. He was just your average, ordinary student."

She stretched out her long fingers and tapped their tips together. "So why all the questions?"

I cleared my voice. "He didn't attend my Friday class either, and I started wondering if it was my assignment that kept him away. Actually, I'm glad to hear he missed your class as well. It makes me feel a great deal better."

"Death by truancy?" Her falsetto laughter echoed through the tiny room.

I attempted to laugh also. "More or less," I managed. "Thanks again," I said and waved goodbye.

Something about the woman bothered me, and I decided it was her long fingers. The way they were always stretching and folding—it was distracting at best, creepy at worst. Despite her finger calisthenics, however, the appointment had been successful. I'd found out that Austin didn't attend her class and consequently hadn't skipped mine because of the poetry assignment. This gave me a small amount of satisfaction, knowing that Austin might have participated had he not had other plans that morning. Those other plans were paramount to finding out what kept him from attending class Friday morning yet brought him to campus.

With my mind on the case, I nearly bumped into Officer Sophie Barnes, who was standing near the entrance.

"I'm sorry. Excuse me … Sophie!" I said. "I'm so sorry. I nearly knocked you down."

"That's okay, Professor Prather. It's a bad place to stop." She tucked something into her pocket.

"I'm glad I ran into you again—not literally, of course—but

I wanted to talk to you the other day. I knew you were busy, though."

She wore a neat brown ponytail that bobbed up and down as she talked. Her brown eyes, too, revealed her excitement as she leaned in so close that I could smell her strawberry shampoo. "This case," she said, her voice barely above a whisper, "it's the most exhilarating thing I've ever worked on. It's all I can think about."

"I'm so happy for you."

"I think it's going to change things around there for me, you know? Instead of being the new college kid, I'm going to be a real cop."

"The next great detective, perhaps?"

At this, she turned sheepish and curbed her enthusiasm. "Oh, Professor Prather, nothing like that. But it *is* the chance I've been looking for. You know what I mean? They just don't take you seriously down there until you prove yourself somehow."

I nodded. "I know what you mean. The entire department thought I was a kook until I was accepted for a conference at Harvard last spring to present my paper on Female Empowerment and the Romantic novel. They thought I'd read all those Harlequins in vain."

She giggled like a young girl.

"You know, I was on my way to lunch just now. Would you like to join me?" I asked.

She turned serious. "Oh, I don't think I should. Beamer wouldn't like it."

"Why not?"

"Well … I don't know." I could see she was looking for a way to tell me without offending me. "The investigation and all. It might not look proper."

"Of course. I wouldn't want to get you in trouble. Just walk with me to my car, then."

Although clouds still populated most of the sky, a ray of mild sunshine peeked through momentarily, like an old friend. I stood for a moment, completely still, feeling the sun soak through my jacket. It felt glorious.

I resumed walking. After a few steps, I asked, "How *is* the case going? Any news?"

Sophie's lips turned up ever so slightly.

"There is …" I said.

"There might be," she replied.

"You know Austin was my student," I said.

She nodded. "I know. Wow! Is this your car?"

"Yes."

"It's cool. What is it?"

"Thank you. It's a '69 Mustang. The news—is it about how Austin died?"

"It's nothing official, Professor Prather. A tox screen can take six weeks to come back."

"But you do know something?" I asked.

"It's a chemical—"

"A poison," I broke in.

She looked around to see if I'd been overheard, but I knew I hadn't been. We were alone in the parking lot.

"I don't know if I should really be telling you this."

"Well, I should think it's a matter of some public importance. And besides, he was my student. That makes it more of my concern."

"I know, but it also makes you a suspect," she whispered.

"A suspect." The word hung in the air. "Was he murdered, then?"

She stood there, biting her bottom lip.

"Listen, Sophie, I don't want you to get in trouble. My students mean a lot to me, and you're one of my former students, too. I just want to know the truth about Austin."

"Here's the deal …" she started.

I knew her Midwestern sensibility would come through in the end.

"The coroner found a chemical in the vic's—sorry, Austin's—

body called ethylene chlorohydrin. I guess it's used for all sorts of things and also as a pesticide. The thing is, we're not sure how Austin came into contact with it."

"A pesticide?" I raised my eyebrows. "I imagine every farmer this side of the state has access to it."

She shook her head. "It makes it difficult; that's for sure."

I began to feel warm, standing in the sun, and very hungry. It was time to get something to eat and let Sophie go on her way.

"Professor Prather, you're not going to tell anyone, are you? You know, it could be nothing. It's not official."

I opened my car door. "You know me, Sophie—always the soul of discretion."

Now it was her turn to raise her eyebrows. "Just keep it between us, okay?"

I got into my Mustang and started it with a rumble. "I promise, Sophie. I would never let you down. You keep yourself safe. It could be that we have a murderer on the loose."

"It doesn't seem possible, does it?" said Sophie, looking around at the quiet town that surrounded us.

As I drove away, I thought it was not only possible but probable. In fact, I was certain now that Austin had been murdered. How else would he have come in contact with such a chemical? There was no doubt in my mind that someone had poisoned him—but how and why? The answers seemed as elusive as Austin himself.

Chapter Fourteen

———

A FTER GRABBING A quick lunch, I stopped by Lenny's house to report what Sophie had told me. I needed to tell someone, soul of discretion or not, and I knew he would not repeat what I said. I had been to his house a couple of times over the last year. In the backyard was an extraordinary willow tree, which hovered over the small ranch house like an overprotective mother.

Like most of the houses on Park Street, his was built in the 1970s. It was olive green and rectangular and very similar in design to the ones surrounding it. Their coherence made the street look neat and organized and gave the impression that nothing out of the ordinary ever happened here. It was a comforting feeling, I reflected as I parked in the single-lane driveway, to stand at one end of the street and see nothing out of place.

From the door, I could hear "Sergeant Pepper's Lonely Hearts Club Band" playing loudly, and I assumed Lenny was grading papers. He told me once that playing music helped keep his mind off all the run-on sentences and that he wouldn't be able to get through a set of papers without John Lennon. Everyone had their methods, I supposed. Mine were altogether different. I preferred to grade papers in absolute silence. And I enjoyed the process of making corrections. I marked each grammatical error with a different color highlighter. Students were expected to memorize the color code at the beginning of the semester: red for comma splices, yellow for run-ons, orange for fragments, and green for misplaced modifiers. Lenny thought they were my replacement for crayons, but I assured him they were not. Indeed, I'd never enjoyed coloring as a child as I didn't have the patience to stay within the lines. In fact, while other girls honed their skills by completing complex coloring books of Strawberry Shortcake, I was busy writing thinly veiled stories about the working families in my neighborhood.

I waited for quite a while before the music stopped and Lenny appeared at the door in lounge pants and a Pepsi t-shirt.

"Oh, it's you," he said. "I thought you were Mrs. Baker. I was trying to come up with a good excuse."

I liked this about Lenny. He never seemed surprised by anything I did, even coming by his house unannounced in the middle of the afternoon.

He held open the door, and I walked in.

"She lives next door. But I'm pretty sure today is Laundromat day."

I wondered how he knew it was laundry day but didn't ask. Instead, I said, "Can I move these?" and after he nodded, took a stack of papers from his recliner and moved them to his keyboard bench so that I could sit down. Lenny not only played keyboard, he also played electric guitar. In fact, he moonlighted with several area bands and was a well-respected musician within the community.

"She hates loud music," he said, "even in the middle of the afternoon." He sat down on his black couch, moving aside the piles of folders and miniature candy wrappers. "So what's up? Austin, right? I can tell by your skyrocketing eyebrows."

I nonchalantly relaxed my face. "I talked to Sophie, the police officer who used to be my student."

"What about Sarah? What happened with her?"

I gestured impatiently. "I'll get back to her."

"It's important that I keep these things in my head chronologically," he said.

"Oh good god Sarah was at the poetry reading that night!" This I spewed out in one long breath, trying to continue before he could stop me.

"Ah ha! He *was* with a girl," he said, slapping his leg.

"We knew that already."

"Yeah, well, we didn't know it was Sarah."

"In fact, she was probably the last one to see him alive before he was *murdered*," I stressed.

"I thought we were ordered to use that word more cautiously."

"After talking to Sophie," I said, "I'm guessing it's a word we'll hear a lot more of."

"I think the term you're looking for is 'involuntary manslaughter.' When that guy in Iowa—"

"Can I just tell you what Sophie said?"

He shrugged. "I can see that you're going to anyway."

"Sophie said that the coroner found a chemical in Austin's body called ethylene chlorohydrin—a poison." I leaned back in the chair, satisfied to have revealed my news.

"No wonder. That is a nugget," said Lenny, putting his hands behind his head. "How is it used?"

"I don't know anything about it, really."

He ran his fingers through his hair until it came to a nearly perfect point at the top of his head. "Does all this really mean Austin was murdered?"

"Come on, Lenny. He couldn't have *accidentally* come in contact with something like that, could he? Somebody had to poison him with it."

The word hung in the air, and neither of us said anything for a moment.

"Well ... there it is," said Lenny.

I nodded silently.

"So what now?" he asked.

I moved to a cross-legged position as I tried to sort out my thoughts. "How would he have come in contact with the chemical? Sophie Barnes said it could be used as a pesticide. I know he told me he lived on a farm, but that was before he came to campus."

"The kid was into everything, as far as I can tell. Theater, ROTC. What about the fraternity? Could some cruel hoax have gone wrong that weekend—a hazing thing?"

I jumped up. "Of course! Where's your laptop?"

"It's right here. Why?"

It was lying on top of another stack of papers. I squeezed in beside him on the couch, opening the computer.

"It's just something you said." I pulled up Google and searched for the chemical. "I want to see if we can find a description on the Internet."

"Look at you. Going all non-academic on me."

I shook my head. "Do you think I have the nerve to search the science databases? I could not begin to decipher that gobbledygook."

After a few misspelled searches, I found a federal poison control website that described ethylene chlorohydrin's properties briefly. I told Lenny, "It's used as all sorts of things: a pesticide, solvent, fabric dye—a degreaser. It smells faintly of ether. It's almost completely undetectable when absorbed by the skin. And listen to this: it has a sweet taste!"

I gave him a good shove as I relayed this fact, but he still looked puzzled. "The fraternity?" I said. "Rush week? Shots of the alcoholic variety?"

"Makes sense. Damn I'm good." He stroked his stubbly chin whiskers.

I shut the laptop. "You *are* good. I'm completely impressed."

He smiled widely, and I suddenly realized how close to him

I was sitting. I could smell his musky cologne. I moved back to my chair, returning the laptop to its appropriate pile.

"I think it's time to pay a call on the fraternity," I said. "Find out what really went on that weekend."

His smile turned into a smirk. How well I knew the difference. "Pay a call on the fraternity. What do you mean? Like, just stop in?"

"I see what you mean. I would certainly need a reason for stopping by, wouldn't I? They are a members-only sort of thing, I suppose. You didn't happen to be—"

"A frat boy? Hell no." He seemed truly disgusted by the notion.

"Well, two frat brothers are in my 101 class. I should be able to ask them a few questions—discreetly, of course."

Now his smirk turned into laughter. "Have you looked up your definition of 'discreet' lately? It has a picture of a lady with a bomb—"

"Ha ha, very funny. I'll have you know that I can be surreptitious when I want to be," I said.

He looked at me quizzically. "Are you trying to raise one eyebrow again? Because it just looks like you got a stray lash in your eye."

I stood up. "I'll keep working on it. In the meantime, I'm going to find a way to get to those fraternity guys. See what really happened that weekend. I'll let you know if I find anything out."

"I'll be waiting on pins and needles."

I reached for the doorknob.

"Hey, be careful though, Em. Promise?"

I looked over my shoulder and crossed my heart. As I walked down the concrete steps, just before I reached my car, I heard "Sergeant Pepper" resume. A small smile escaped my lips. There were many reasons I liked Lenny, and this was one of them: for him, life *moved*. And he always moved with it. He did not overthink situations, even this one; he was someone who got things done.

Chapter Fifteen

—

THE MORE I learned about Austin, and the more preoccupied I became with his murder, the more I allowed the obligations of my day-to-day routine to slip. I found myself petting Dickinson and staring out the window a good deal now, allowing my unfinished research and unwashed dishes to pile up like the leaves outside my window. The difference was that a nice big wind wouldn't come and blow my obligations away. I would need to do the work. Thinking, however hard, about the murder did not constitute work. I should have been writing a chapter on the French lovers Abelard and Heloise, examining how letter writing allowed Heloise a creative outlet in the twelfth century. It was to be part of a larger book that examined early alternative spaces for female authors, a book that might bring me closer to tenure. But now the completion of that book seemed as far away as the warm days of summer.

I stood up and put down the cat. As I glanced through the neat stacks of research in my study, I was still thinking about the murder. I barely knew Austin, yet somehow I felt responsible. I needed to find out the truth about his death and finish this story, *his* story. It was the only one that mattered to me right now.

I went to the kitchen, poured myself another cup of coffee, and then left it on the counter. It was almost eight o'clock Friday morning, and I needed to get ready for my composition class. It had been two days, and I still hadn't thought of an excuse to visit the fraternity. Maybe something would occur to me in lecture. At the very least, I could ask one or both of the fraternity boys about initiation. I was headed for the shower when a sudden recollection of my meeting with the arts committee made me pause and return for my coffee. The meeting would give me the perfect opportunity to ask questions without appearing nosy. Encouraged, I stepped into the shower. Today wasn't going to be that bad after all.

I WALKED BY St. Agnes Church because a local chapter of the Catholic Daughters met there regularly to bake and talk and pray. If the French had the market on pastries, the Catholic Daughters had the market on bars and cookies. At least in my book. The gooey caramel, the semi-sweet chocolate, the fresh walnuts, the shaved coconut—every confection was a reason to sing glory to God in the highest. I needed only to close my eyes, and I could recall the soft, plump hands of the ladies— mostly older, though a few were young—stirring, shaping, baking. It was nothing for them to bake twelve dozen cookies before nine. Someone was always dying, about to die, or ready to give birth, and fresh cookies were always welcome. And then there were the St. Agnes School kids. They got some too, if they were good, and if they said their Hail Marys.

The women were never stingy with me, though I usually only attended Mass when I went home to Detroit. They knew my fondness for sweets, and the moment Arlis, a large Norwegian woman, saw me coming, she immediately dusted off her hands, cut me a seven-layer bar, and pointed me in the direction of the coffee pot. Just as I used to do with my own mother, I sat near the women watching them, thinking to myself how *good* they were, these quiet women who made the church go round. When they finished and sat down with their rosaries, I listened reverently. I figured this was as close to religion as I would get these days and blessed myself as I left.

As usual I admired the edifice as I passed by, the discolored orangish brick and the three stained-glass windows, each displaying a scene from Jesus's birth. The idea that something could be so rugged and yet so beautiful appealed to me, and I found myself using the church as a symbol for the entire town, although I'm sure the Presbyterians would have objected.

I quickened my step. I needed all the time I could get to review the short stories by Flannery O'Connor, who was, incidentally, also a Catholic but one I could not reconcile with the ladies from the church. The students liked her mean characters and their funny clothes, so I always included a few of her stories in the literary unit. Yet I hadn't managed to force myself to re-read them the previous evening in the peace of the fall moon. Now I would need to skim them quickly and mark passages with my highlighter before class.

I went straight to my classroom in Stanton Hall. I wanted space to think and sunlight to sit in. My office afforded me neither. I could ask for no better accommodations on this morning, feeling sad that the police had made no more progress on Austin's murder. The room was quiet; the sunlight stretched out her long fingers to warm the corners of the foggy windows, and the light blue sky made the day appear milder than it was.

I opened my book to the case study on Flannery O'Connor and began scanning. It wasn't long before I remembered she had lupus and died fairly young, and then my thoughts strayed to Austin and why it should be that some people got to live a long time and others not long at all. I blinked slowly, turned to keep the sun from crisscrossing my eyelashes, and refocused on the text. The letters seemed not to create sentences but words that didn't come together in any meaningful way. I let out a sigh, which sounded so loud and foreign that it startled me. I looked up, expecting to see a student, perhaps Austin, seated in the back row, but there was no one. Just four empty chairs, like all the others, placed one next to the other behind the wooden desks.

I walked out of the classroom toward the water fountain and took a drink. It was time for class. This was one place I must close the door on my melancholy. I straightened my shoulders and walked back into the room.

A few students walked in, cheeks pink from the cold. I was glad to see Jared was not in class. His absence would give me a chance to question Adam—a pretty good kid when Jared wasn't around—about the fraternity.

After taking attendance, I slipped my grade book back into my bag and organized the students into small groups. They would have more interesting things to say about O'Connor than I did, so I dismissed my prepared lecture and sat back to watch them work, waiting for an opportunity to talk to Adam. He was a good-looking kid, the kind who would fit in easily with the fraternity. His style was less obvious than Jared's, but he had a nice face and fashionable hair. He was busily taking notes for his group and making sense of their comments. He would be the one to speak—being probably the best prepared—so naturally he took a greater interest in the conversation. A sophomore girl in his group had lots to say about the story while a freshman girl doodled. The other boy in his group seemed completely unorganized and only spoke when spoken to.

I walked around the room, contributing here and there to the various conversations to avoid making an obvious beeline for Adam's group.

"Is the group all set?" I said, looking over the shoulder of the young girl who was drawing miniature cat faces on her notebook.

"Yep. Yes we are," said Adam.

"Good," I said. "And how are *you* doing?"

"Me?" said Adam.

The girl looked up from her cat.

"This must be a difficult time for you," I said, awkwardly patting his shoulder. "I know Austin was in your fraternity."

"He wasn't in yet," he said.

I pretended to look puzzled. It was a look I had perfected from years of hearing elaborate stories from students as to why their papers were late.

"He was still a pledge."

I kept my look blank, but I knew what a pledge was. During this time, a pledge would get to know the fraternity members, do various odd jobs for them if asked, learn the Greek alphabet. Ultimately, the pledge was pledging his loyalty and trust to the fraternity and might have undergone any number of challenges that tested his devotion to the brotherhood. What I wanted to know was if one of these challenges had resulted in Austin's death.

Adam said, "He hadn't been inducted yet."

"Of course," I said, my expression clearing. "I suppose he was subject to various drinking contests and these sorts of things." I was hoping he would confirm my suspicions that alcohol was involved, a substance that could have easily masked the taste of the chemical.

"Something like that," he said.

I looked over his notebook. "Very thoughtful response there. I think you're absolutely right about O'Connor." He smiled at my compliment. "So … did he win? The contest, I mean?"

Adam furrowed his brow. "It wasn't really a contest. We had a party Friday to celebrate everybody's week of challenges. "

"Well, that sounds like fun. I suppose you partied all night."

He seemed to be thinking back to that night. "Yeah, pretty much. Austin left early, though." He laughed. "Jared was kind of pissed about that."

"Pissed?" I said. I supposed Jared would have preferred him to pass out on the floor.

"Sorry," Adam said immediately. He probably thought the language offended me. "Really, he was probably just jealous that Austin had a girlfriend and he didn't. The girls dug Austin. That farm boy thing really worked for him."

I looked around, satisfied that the groups still buzzed with conversation. "Oh yeah? Someone you know?"

He shook his head. "No. I didn't get a look at her. She didn't want to come in."

I wondered if this mystery girl was Sarah. Perhaps she didn't want to take the chance of word getting back to Sean. Then a thought occurred to me. "How do you know it was a girl then?"

Adam shrugged. "I don't know, I guess. He just said it was."

"Oh. I see." I looked around the room. Discussions had given way to giddy chaos. It was time to reconvene the class. I moved back to the podium, hushed the students, and began calling on groups. Still, my mind kept drifting back to Adam and Jared and Austin. Adam had said Jared was angry that Austin left early; certainly that wasn't reason enough to poison him. Maybe Jared was jealous of Austin or his girlfriend. Austin was different and that made him popular, at least with the girls. Jared seemed to be the most influential, if not popular, boy at his fraternity. I couldn't imagine boyhood jealousy being a motive for murder, but then again, I didn't understand the hierarchy of fraternities. If only there were some way to get more information about the fraternity itself. I didn't dare pose any more questions in future classes, especially after Jared returned.

After the bell rang, I literally ran into Claudia, who was coming up the stairs and talking with a student who had more of her attention than the stairs did.

"Beth, I'll see you tomorrow. Em, I want to talk to you." Claudia did a full circle and began walking down the stairs with me.

"Hey, Claudia. How are you? How is Gene?"

"Gene is Gene," she said, shaking her head. "He's living downstairs. I cannot abide him in my living space right now."

How she'd convinced a grown man to live in his own basement was beyond me, but I nodded anyway as if there were nothing unusual about the arrangement.

"But this isn't about Gene. This is about Sarah Sorenson. She said you interrogated her before class the other day."

"She said that?" I said, holding the door for her.

She tossed her head. We were outside the building now, and the breeze was stirring her hair. "She didn't say that, exactly, but I know you, Em, and you're on a witch hunt. I can tell from your lips. They're twitching all the time."

Instinctively, I put my hand to my mouth.

"I know you mean well, and I have nothing against you personally for trying to find answers to your student's death, but as a representative of this sacred society—"

"You mean the university, right?" I interrupted.

"Yes, as a representative of the *university*, you must not succumb to your own whims. You must put the students first."

I couldn't believe Claudia was telling me I couldn't succumb to my whims. Her whims were the basis for her entire creative writing curriculum. "I'm sorry if Sarah was upset by our conversation. She didn't seem to be at the time. She should be upset that her boyfriend is dead. Now that's something to get upset about."

Claudia twisted her hair into a bun and secured it with a pencil. "See, it's that kind of attitude that I'm talking about. Austin wasn't her boyfriend. Even if he was, Gene could drop dead this very instant and I wouldn't shed a tear—not one tear—and he's my husband. You don't know how these men are, Em. They're absolute death sentences."

I was somewhat insulted. I dated plenty of guys in college, but the dates never produced any long-term relationships, which might have been more my fault than theirs. When I was an undergraduate, I belonged to a book club that sent me five new historical romance novels and a rose-colored wine glass in each shipment. This routine ensured that a man would need to wear a kilt—or at least a well-woven cravat—to be worthy of my love. "Hey, that's not fair. I've dated my share of death sentences. What about Ricky Anderson?"

Claudia fiddled with her bun. "Who?"

I threw up my hands. "You know? That guy I dated over the summer so enamored with his high school days that he still wore his letterman jacket on our dates? The Lincoln Lion Cat?"

"Oh, him. He was a piece of work. I'm not saying he wasn't a piece of work because he was. But he wasn't a death sentence. They can't be death sentences until you've married them."

Conversations with Claudia were exhausting, and I found my mind floating away on a little white cloud passing overhead. She was still talking, but I was no longer listening.

"And that could mean trouble for you."

I refocused on Claudia. "What could mean trouble?"

She stopped directly in front of the rose garden. It smelled overly sweet and out of place.

"Your questioning. Your meddling. Your reputation. You'll go from quirky to downright ... *strange*!"

Now I smiled. Was Claudia actually worried about me? "I won't harass any more of your students if that's what this is about. I promise."

"Em, it's not just about that—although I am their chief advocate. It's about *you*."

Before I could be completely convinced of her concern, she had her hand on her forehead, shielding her eyes from the sun.

"There's Owen Jorgenson. Now there's a husband I wouldn't mind having. They always say you should marry a man at least ten years your elder. Ann took that advice, but *I* just had to go out and marry the first piece of garbage I took up with." She waved at him, and he waved back. "He attends absolutely everything with her—without a straitjacket. And he's in the *science* department."

I nodded eagerly. "I know. He was Austin's science teacher. It was in the student newspaper."

"*Zip it about Austin*," she hissed. Then her voice turned silky. "Owen! Nice to see you."

In his early forties, Owen was a substantial man with broad shoulders and sandy blond hair. His eyes crinkled when he smiled.

"Hello, Claudia. Hi, Emmeline."

"Hey, Owen," I said.

"The poetry slam was a big hit last Friday, Claudia," Owen said. "There were a lot of talented writers there. Ann and I enjoyed ourselves thoroughly."

Claudia beamed, gathering his praise like petals, and I quickly took the opportunity to ask Owen about Austin. Claudia shot me a disappointed look, but I pretended not to notice.

"Austin Oliver? What an ordeal, right? I was shocked. Just shocked." He shook his head as if he were still as puzzled as on the day he heard the news. "Anyway, did he miss class? No, he never missed. He was a decent kid. Always helping set up lab on Wednesdays. I think he had a real aptitude for science, do you know?"

"Well that explains why he didn't like my English class," I said.

"Oh, I'm sure that's not true, but I *was* supposed to meet with him about the science major. Very few science majors like English and vice versa, you know."

"Which is why it's so wonderful to see you at so many of our events," Claudia said, trying to regain control of the conversation.

"So you never met with him?" I asked.

He shook his head slowly. "No, I never did. In fact, he wanted to meet with me earlier, but I didn't have time. I had an interview in Minneapolis. We were going to meet on Monday ...." The end of his sentence drifted off into the mild breeze. He shook his head, clearly disgusted with himself. "It's a shame. His last impression of me was that I was too busy for him."

"That's not true," said Claudia. "You inspired him so much that he wanted to pursue your profession. That is something you can be very proud of. Not every teacher can say that," she added, glancing at me.

"So you're looking into a different campus?" I asked politely.

"Ann thinks she would have more opportunities," said Owen.

"She's probably right," said Claudia. "Our Women's Department can hardly be called a department."

He readjusted his bag on his shoulder and glanced at his watch. "She always is. But I'd have a heck of a time leaving this place. I've lived here my whole life; the land is in my blood. Oh well, change is a good thing, right? That's what everyone says, anyway."

"It's food for the soul," Claudia agreed enthusiastically.

"I'm going to go get some food for the stomach right now, so I'd better hustle. Ann's meeting me. If you'd like to join us, you're both welcome." He looked from Claudia to me.

"I've got office hours and then a committee meeting," I said.

"And I've got an appointment off campus, but soon. We'll get together soon," added Claudia.

"I'm sure I'll see you at your next reading," he said to Claudia. "Keep us posted."

"Always," said Claudia cheerfully.

He was barely a foot away from us when her voice turned stony. "Do you think that was really necessary? You nearly had the poor man in tears."

I rolled my eyes. "Not even close."

"Heed my warning, Emmeline ..." she said.

I silently prepared myself for more inflated language.

"Otherwise you'll be the next one looking for a new job."

I stared after her as she stomped away, surprised by her vigor. Claudia was Claudia, but really! I hardly thought my job was in jeopardy. That was going too far even for her.

Chapter Sixteen

———

I HAD OFFICE hours scheduled before the committee meeting on *Les Mis*, so I went to my office and waited impatiently for my computer to start. I was still irritated with Claudia—and academia in general. This wasn't a time for scholastic floundering; it was a time for action. How she could have the audacity to question my questioning was beyond me. A student was dead—*my* student—and if a death didn't constitute a call to action, I didn't know what did.

Owen Jorgenson's class had proven to be inconsequential, as it didn't meet on Fridays, so I had little there to pursue. Still, Owen had said something important—that Austin enjoyed science and had an aptitude for it. Adam's revelation could also be key. Austin had been drinking at the frat party on Friday, the night before he died. I needed to find out what had happened that night, and if there was a chance Austin ingested the chemical at the party.

Although I didn't know much about fraternities, I knew quite a bit about dorm rooms, having been a part of university life since I was a student myself. I knew almost anything could be found out by just asking a person's roommate, who often held at least a detached interest in their roomie's welfare. I double-clicked on the Internet icon and waited a few more seconds for the browser to launch. On the university's intranet, I pulled up my Composition 101 class roster. I found out his adviser (Ann Jorgenson), his major (undeclared), and his dorm room (twenty-two) just by drilling down on his name. I scrolled over "Oliver" and clicked. He had been housed in Vanderwood, a co-ed freshmen dorm, before his death, and I wondered if his room had been blocked off for police investigation or if it was still occupied by his roommate. Knowing the university's preference for full houses, I predicted the room would still be in use.

I looked at the clock. Although my office hours weren't officially over, no one had stopped in, and I didn't have any appointments scheduled. If I left now, I would have time to visit the dorms, but not for lunch too. I rummaged through my coin jar, looking for quarters but finding dimes. The junk food in the vending machine was getting more expensive every year. I fondly remembered the days when I could buy a Snickers for fifty cents. Now I would be lucky to get a pack of Lifesavers for that.

I shoved several coins in my pocket and locked the door behind me. For a moment, I stood absolutely still, struck with a desire to go through Windsor Hall. I shook my head. There was no reason to go that way. The meeting wasn't until three o'clock, and the vending machine was directly downstairs.

I decided on a Salted Nut Roll and proceeded out the back door of Harriman Hall. The Vanderwood dorms were behind our building and faced the parking lot. As the fall air entered my lungs, a thought entered my mind. This was the exact place I had overheard the conversation between Austin and the girl the night of the English Department potluck. Though I tried to recap the evening's conversation in my head, the only thing I could remember was the woman's threat. Austin wanted a woman to tell someone something—he wanted it badly. But who and what? Sarah was the first girl who came to my mind. Maybe he wanted her to tell Sean about their relationship, to make it official. It made sense.

I continued toward Vanderwood. The freshmen dorms were not our campus's best feature; they were small, dark, and old. How any eighteen-year-old could manage to stay in one an entire year was beyond me, but most did, though I'd heard more complaining this year than last. They were due for a remodel, that was certain, I thought as I pulled open the front door. If the sherbet-orange paint wasn't enough to repel students, the sea-foam green furniture most certainly was.

"Your ID, I said!" a student yelled from behind a desk, and I turned around and looked behind me, not realizing at first that she was talking to me.

"Of course, you need a university ID. Well, let me just find you one here," I said, rummaging through my oversized purse. "Here's my library card," I mumbled. "I suppose that won't work. I've been looking for that for … oh here it is! It's me with shorter hair. I really prefer it, don't you? When it's long, it's constantly blowing in my face."

The student's tight-lipped smile seemed to say, "Please move on. You're bothering me."

"Thank you. I'm just going up to room twenty-two. Don't worry, I'll find it," I added, though the girl didn't budge an inch in my direction. She went back to her book without so much as a polite nod of the head.

I assumed room twenty-two was on the second floor, since the girls and boys were usually separated by floors, and several females sat chatting or working on laptops on the first floor. I also assumed that room twenty-two was not off limits because the student downstairs hadn't objected when I mentioned the number. Perhaps it *was* still in use by Austin's roommate. Walking up the short staircase, I realized that I needed to come up with an explanation for being there—and soon. The door of the room before me looked just like the others, no yellow police tape in sight.

Before I had a chance to knock (or find the right avenue of exploration), a young man flung open the door. Stunned, I stood with my mouth open, not moving. The student nearly knocked me over, but he stopped short, balancing on his toes like a tipsy ballerina.

"Hey ... sorry," he said. His angry eyes relaxed a bit when he realized I was not a student.

"Not at all," I said, quickly recovering. "I hope I'm not interrupting."

"No, I was just on my way out."

"Well, I won't keep you long. I just have a few questions about Austin. He was your roommate?"

"Oh, sure." He let his skateboard fall to the floor. He'd had this conversation before. "He was a good guy. I liked him."

"You were friends, then?" I asked.

"No. Not really. He wasn't into skating. I don't know what he was into. He wasn't around much. Neither am I."

I nodded. Not all college roommates ended up being best friends. Not even most. "The night before Austin ... died, he went out with some guys from a fraternity. When he came back, did he appear sick?"

He looked thoughtful for a moment. "I don't think so. I know he was rushing them .... Are you with the cops?"

"Oh no. I was his English teacher," I said offhandedly. "What time did he return?"

He looked bewildered by my line of questioning. "I don't know. Midnight? I'd just got back myself."

"I know he had been drinking, but did he stumble or vomit or behave in a suspicious way?"

"He just went to bed."

"Hmm," I said, trying to extend this answer. I picked at something sticky on my sweater, which must have fallen from my Salted Nut Roll.

He kicked at his skateboard.

I smiled.

He added, "He must not have been too sick, though. He woke up at the crack of dawn the next morning."

"Was that unusual?" I asked.

"Hell no! I mean, no. That's the one thing I hated about him. He got up every day around six o'clock. Said it was an old habit from the farm. It annoyed me."

With a sympathetic smile, I said, "Those early birds, who can stand them? So, did he seem the same that morning? Or was he hung over?"

"He was fine as far as I could tell. I didn't get up."

I nodded toward his skateboard. "I see you have somewhere to go. I won't delay you any further. Thank you so much for your time."

He smiled shyly. "Oh … well … thank you, Professor …?"

I smiled back. "You are welcome. Have a good skate."

Chapter Seventeen

—

THE COMMITTEE MET in Windsor again, but this time, the group was rather subdued. After all, it had been only six days since Austin died in the theater, and nobody was as excited about the play as they had been two weeks ago.

It was three o'clock, and the air was stale from inactivity. The narrow vault of the ceiling made the small room feel even smaller and the silence heavier. We were all waiting for Alex, though no one said as much. Jane was reading a journal, Rita was scanning a handout, Dan was looking out the window, and Ann was flipping through a magazine. I dug through the stuff at the bottom of my purse and found my cellphone. Unfortunately, it was out of battery life, and now I had nothing to do but wait.

I caught Dan's eye when there was a noise at the door we thought might be Alex. But it was just someone passing by.

Dan barely smiled, but it was enough for me to start a conversation with him.

"Have you heard any more from Officer Beamer?" I asked.

Everyone looked at Dan, who glanced around the room before answering.

"No. I saw that girl who was with him, though," said Dan. "She searched the theater again. She seems to think Austin left behind a clue to his death."

"I'm sure she's right," said Rita, returning to her handout. "Something in there killed him. The sooner you find out the better ... before the killer strikes again."

Dan looked shocked by her statement, but she didn't notice—or care.

"Did she say what she was looking for?" asked Ann.

"No, she didn't," Dan said. "But I think maybe it was an article of clothing. She asked where he kept his belongings."

"Of course," I said. Sophie was on to the gloves.

Now everyone was staring at me, so I returned to Dan. "And then what?"

"That's all, I guess. I got the feeling she thought I knew more than I was telling her, but that wasn't so. I told her everything I knew."

"I'm sure you did," said Jane. "The police are treating everyone like suspects. It's ridiculous."

"He died in the theater—that's true—but that doesn't mean a theater person or even a person killed him. He might have had asthma or some underlying condition ...." Dan's sentence drifted off.

"He was healthy as a horse as far as I could determine from the newspaper article," added Rita. She was busy making corrections on her handout.

"One never knows," said Jane. "He could have been on drugs for all we know. Meth. It's huge in the Midwest. Huge."

"That sounds like bullshit," said Rita. "Wasn't he in ROTC?"

"Yes, he was in ROTC," I said.

"Sure he was. They don't let a kid with asthma in ROTC," said Rita.

"Did you know him well, Emmeline?" asked Jane. "Your interview wasn't mentioned in the article."

"Yes, I did. *Quite* well." I said this only to spite Jane. "He was beginning to regard me as a confidante."

Ann looked back and forth between me and Jane. "But they really don't know what happened to him, do they?" she said. "It could have been any number of things."

Now Rita put down her pencil. "If I were a betting woman, I'd bet what killed him is in the theater. That's all I'm saying."

"Well I'm glad we got that out of the way," said Alex as he breezed into the room. "A student is dead. It's terrible. It's sad. It's unfortunate. But it doesn't have anything to do with my theater. That I can assure you." Here he looked directly at Rita, but she was unfazed. "We have a play to produce in less than six weeks; that is the subject at hand. So unless anyone has anything else they would like to add, I would like to move on to the play."

I certainly did, and I certainly wanted to, if only for Rita's sake. But we all kept quiet.

"Oh good," said Alex. "I'm so glad we can move on."

And move on we did. We moved through all the items on the agenda within forty-five minutes. Alex appeared disgusted with us for even discussing Austin's death. To him it was petty gossip that was undermining his play, and in some respect, I could see where he was coming from. If the death continued to be the focus of the theater, his production would suffer, and for a narcissist like Alex that would be devastating.

When we cut out early, Jane looked crestfallen. She'd been counting on having the opportunity to discuss Medieval Mondays. The rest of us were relieved. The committee hadn't been the artistic collaboration it had been last year, and I was glad my two-year commitment would be fulfilled in the spring. After the group dispersed, Ann and I walked down the hall to her office. She turned on the light and flung her purse onto the chair.

"I'm glad that's over," she said.

"Me, too," I said, taking the other free chair.

"Didn't you think Alex was just a bit over the top? It's not like he holds some special title in the group."

"I agree. And I certainly do not want him speaking for the rest of us if that's going to continue to be his attitude."

"I know. Right?" Ann said, clicking on a desk lamp. "It's like he's mad that that kid died in the theater."

"Can you believe the audacity of it?" I said, shaking my head. Jane passed Ann's room on the way to the English Department. I smiled briefly as Jane's eyes met mine. She waved and kept walking.

Ann raised her eyebrows. "Speaking of audacity …."

I chuckled. "I know."

"Well, anyways, I was sorry to hear he was in your class. I know you're pretty close to your students."

"Thank you," I said, growing serious again. "I don't think I'd be exaggerating if I said his death has turned my life upside down."

She nodded sympathetically. "I completely understand. I would feel the same way if one of my students had an accident."

I wanted to say that I didn't think his death was an accident, but after Claudia's warning, I thought it better to refrain. Instead I smiled and switched topics. "So, I heard Owen had an interview in Minneapolis? You must be positively thrilled."

She leaned forward. "Thrilled isn't the word. If they really want him, they'll find something for me, too. Do you know how many faculty they have in their Women's Studies program?" She didn't wait for my answer. "Eighteen! Eighteen people make a real department last time I checked."

"That's larger than our English Department," I said.

"I know. Cross your fingers."

I stood up. "I can do better than that. I'll light a candle for you at St. Agnes."

She laughed. "I didn't know you were Catholic."

I shrugged. "I used to be, but I'm seriously considering rejoining just to get in on the bake sale."

"See you later," Ann called as I walked out and turned toward the English Department. I tiptoed across the narrow passageway that connected the two buildings, certain that one day I would fall right through.

Jane was talking to Giles outside his door, which was also just outside my office. I tried to enter with as little commotion as possible, but since my keychain was twice the size it should have been, they heard me.

"And that was it, right, Emmeline? He just dissolved the meeting without one mention of Medieval Mondays," said Jane.

"We'll meet again," I said noncommittally.

"I think he was just annoyed with Rita and all that talk about the theater. It was embarrassing," she said to Giles. He looked at me for confirmation.

"He might have been irritated with her, but we covered everything on the agenda. Besides, he and Rita are really good friends." She would know this if she had been in the group more than a few weeks.

"Well it's one less thing off your plate, right? Now you can get back to more important tasks—like grading your students' papers." Giles looked at me so directly that one would think he'd seen the stack gathering dust on my dining-room table.

"They *are* our number one priority," said Jane, oblivious to the silent exchange between Giles and me.

I went inside my office and packed up my belongings. This weekend I would hit the grading hard. I would finish every paper, good and bad, and bring them back Monday morning. I wouldn't think about Austin or the murder or the theater. I would think of only those students who could still use my help.

As I shut and locked my door, I saw Thomas Cook, the avant-garde researcher of cereal boxes, do the same. His new office was two doors down from mine.

"Have a good weekend," I said as I approached the stairwell.

"Any plans?" he asked.

"Nothing special," I said, not wanting to admit that I had an overdue appointment with a bottle of French wine. "You?"

He tossed his shiny leather satchel over his shoulder. "No. I need to finish a conference proposal."

I turned toward the staircase.

"Emmeline ... I was going to ask you something." He caught up with me.

"Yes?" I said.

"I read in the student newspaper that Austin Oliver was your student."

"Yes, he was," I said. We walked down the staircase together.

"You never mentioned it that day at the theater," said Thomas.

"I guess it didn't come up. You were in a hurry to get out of there, if I remember correctly."

"If you remember *correctly*, I had class," he said. He swept the thick hair out of his eyes.

He was smart and direct. No insinuations would get by him without a rebuttal.

"Anyway, I wanted to ask you what Austin was like." He held open the outside door for me.

"In what way do you mean?" I asked.

"I mean, was there anything about him that seemed peculiar? Unusual? Was he ill-tempered?"

I stopped mid-path. "Ill-tempered? Not at all. Why would you think so?"

"I read something recently in a well-received journal that claims ill-tempered people—even young ones—tend to come to violent ends."

I didn't need a well-received journal to come to that conclusion. Besides, how did he know Austin's end had been violent? "The university has deemed his death accidental."

"Accidents are inherently violent. Wouldn't you agree?"

I began walking again. His was the type of academic discussion that annoyed me. "I suppose. Why are you interested?"

"I just told you. It would be primary research supporting this journal's hypothesis."

"Well, I'm sorry to be a killjoy," I said, my voice sterner, "but Austin was not an ill-tempered student. He was from a local farm."

His cheekbones grew sharper. "There is a substantial amount of violence that takes place on farms. Animals, for instance. It takes a certain temperament to kill another living thing."

Thomas Cook didn't know the difference between a pig farm and a soybean farm. "Perhaps he milked one too many cows in his previous life, and he was secretly seething inside," I said.

His face relaxed. "You are mocking me."

I smiled. "No, I'm not. I promise. It's just been one of those weeks."

"I get it. You are upset by his death. I should have thought of that, and I apologize."

"No apology necessary."

He shoved his hands into his jacket pockets. "It seems we keep getting off on the wrong foot. First you, now me."

At the recollection of the faculty potluck, I internally cringed. How he had the moxie to bring it up, I did not know, but I was gaining a new respect for him. "Well, I guess we're even now."

We approached the edge of the campus, and he turned to say goodbye. He stuck out his hand. "Clean slate?"

"Clean slate," I said, shaking his hand.

"Have a good weekend, Emmeline."

"You also," I said and turned toward my street.

Chapter Eighteen

IF I ANTICIPATED Friday mornings because of the Catholic Daughters, I anticipated Friday evenings even more for the late-night movies on the Public Broadcasting channel. It was really the only time I turned on the TV, except to hear the morning news. I had an entire ritual that began with takeout from Vinny's, my favorite Italian restaurant, a bottle of Bordeaux from Variety Liquors, and an enormous piece of chocolate cake from Sweet Nothings. The dessert I picked up first, since the store closed at five o'clock. A middle-aged woman name Debbie always waited for me—I think almost counted on me—to arrive every Friday just before five. We visited for the five minutes it took her to package the cake in a Styrofoam box; she was especially interested in hearing about any news at the college. Years before, she had worked in the college bookstore and was fascinated with campus gossip. I, too, looked forward to this visit. We were friends in a way.

After picking up the cake and wine, I immediately went for the bathtub, turning up my Édith Piaf CD as loud as I could so I could hear it through the bathroom door. "*Non, je ne regrette rien*" (No, I regret nothing) was my all-time favorite French song, and Piaf's voice seemed perfect for expressing every soul-wrenching experience I'd ever had or imagined.

It was almost seven o'clock, yet light shone faintly through the blinds on the bathroom window, the stray rays making cool shadows on the warm bathroom wall. Soon it would grow winter-dark and seem like the middle of the night at this time of day, but for right now, I could still imagine it was summer and I had nothing to do but listen to my CD and read the latest Jackie Onassis biography.

I was pruny by the time I emerged from the tub and donned my fuzzy yellow robe. The CD had finished, and the house was quiet, except for the sound of a whip-poor-will calling from the backyard. I pulled the phonebook from atop the fridge, and several coupons tumbled to the floor. I searched for one from Vinny's, but the restaurant rarely gave coupons. The food was relatively cheap as it was.

I called in my order of chicken parmesan and Caesar salad and hurried to get dressed. I checked the TV listing: *Rear Window*. Oh, this was going to be good.

Thirty minutes later, I returned with my chicken, piping hot, and poured it onto a large dinner plate along with my salad. Heading into the living room, I balanced the plate in one hand and a wine glass in the other. The cake would be eaten later.

"Don't touch it," I told Dickinson as she stealthily made her way to the coffee table where I had placed the food. She crouched beneath the table, switching her tail back and forth.

The movie was just beginning, and I placed the plate on my lap and turned up the TV. The chicken was perfect, crispy but not overdone, and the sauce spicy and thick. The bread was hot and soft and drizzled with an enchanting butter-garlic sauce. I took a bite and closed my eyes. God could keep heaven as long as I could keep Vinny's.

A loud *thud* interrupted Jimmy Stewart's intimate conversation with Grace Kelly, and I jumped. Then I remembered I had left my open container of chicken parmesan on the kitchen countertop.

"Dickinson, get down from there!" I hollered, my eyes never leaving the television. From below the coffee table, I heard shuffling. Dickinson had fallen asleep on the napkins that had slipped beneath the coffee table and was nowhere near the kitchen. I grabbed the remote control and pressed "mute." All was quiet, except for the sound of the refrigerator. I unmuted the television and returned to the show, but I was still half listening for the noise. Fifteen minutes later, when Mr. Thorwald began bringing out paper parcels in the middle of the night, I heard the *thud* again, louder now. This time I stood up, as if standing would make my ears work better. Dickinson still lay under the table, but now she looked up as if she, too, were questioning the presence of someone else in the room. Cats were always willing to oblige a person if it meant personal duress.

The scene with Mr. Thorwald was even more menacing without the benefit of sound. Silence can be paralyzing under the right circumstances, and my heart was beating louder and louder in my chest. I eventually turned toward the kitchen, picking up my butter knife in the process.

Despite my efforts to balance all my weight on one big toe then the other, the floorboards crackled and popped with each carefully considered step. If indeed someone were in the room, he or she would already know I was coming from the muting of the TV or the shadows on the wall. I walked into the kitchen and flipped on the light. Nothing. The chicken and wine still sat on the counter; the takeout bag still lay on the floor next to the garbage can. It was probably a squirrel or another cat. There were dozens of squirrels and cats that roamed freely at night in this neighborhood, and that thud had sounded just like the sound Dickinson made when she jumped from the kitchen counter. I bent down to pick up the takeout bag and shove it into the garbage can. As I did, I noticed a shape in the crepuscular light of the back alley.

I immediately flicked off the kitchen switch, but it was too late. I could see nothing but the yellow floodlights that shone above Mrs. Gunderson's garage.

Mrs. Gunderson told me once that lights were the biggest deterrent to thieves. They wouldn't go near a house with lights. She'd heard it on the radio. "Ladies alone, living by themselves like you and me, should have lights on. All the time. Lots and lots of lights." We'd had this conversation one day when I mentioned the ever-present lights not only attracted mosquitoes but also kept me awake half the night when my curtain was open to catch the cool nighttime breezes. "That's silly, Emmeline. Nobody keeps their windows open at night. If they do, they can expect to catch a fever. That's what they'll catch." This despite the ninety-degree weather.

Now I coveted Mrs. Gunderson's floodlights. I wished I had installed a pair, at least above my garage in the alley, for I could have made out the shape and determined if it was a man or a woman creeping around my house. The thought brought goose bumps to my arms. Had the person really been so close as to make me believe he or she was in my kitchen? Had the person actually been in my kitchen?

I shut the shades. Certainly not. Certainly no one would have any business in my kitchen. I had nothing anyone could possibly want. I told myself this as I looked around with new eyes, searching for evidence of an intruder. None existed.

I pulled a glass out of the cupboard and filled it with water. There *was* one thing I had, one thing that made me dangerous: suspicions about Austin's death. Of course this was it; it had to be.

I dialed Lenny's number, and surprisingly he answered even though it was Friday night. "Oh. Hi, Lenny. It's me, Em."

"Ms. Prather. This is something new. I'm starting to wonder if you don't have a bit of a crush on me," he said.

"Listen, I think someone was inside my house just now. I just saw him leave by the alley. Or her. I think he was looking for something."

"Jesus, Em. I'll be right there."

"No. You don't need to come over. I just wanted to say ... Lenny?" It figured. He had hung up. So like a man to come to the rescue at the exact time you didn't need him. I set the phone back on the receiver and looked at the remaining chicken parmesan. There was no use wrapping it up now. It would be gone before morning.

Instead, I slipped into my sandals, carelessly tossed in front of the door, and rummaged for my flashlight under the kitchen sink. It didn't surprise me that it wasn't there. It wasn't in the bread drawer either, which was the other place I stashed it if I was in a hurry. Then it dawned on me: it was on my nightstand. After lying awake one night staring at Mrs. Gunderson's well-placed lights, I resorted to childish retribution and stuck the flashlight out my bedroom window, shining it directly on what I hoped was Mrs. Gunderson's bedroom window. Our houses were separated only by a small walkway that entered my backyard. If it was her window, however, she never mentioned it, despite the fact that I repeated the exercise five nights in a row. Sleep deprivation could make a person extraordinarily brazen.

Just as I picked up the flashlight, I heard Lenny banging on the door.

"Jeez, it's open already," I said, giving it a yank.

"What are you doing with your doors wide open?" said Lenny, coming in and poking his head in and out of various rooms. "You're a sitting duck in here."

"Yes, do come in. Please, feel free to search my house. Can I get you anything?"

Now Lenny stopped and looked at me quizzically. "Your hair …."

Instinctively, I smoothed a few curls I had been twisting around my fingers during the movie. "I've been in the bath."

"It's nice."

I felt a ridiculous blush rising in my cheeks.

He sharpened his gaze. "What's the flashlight for?"

"I was on my way outside to see if there were any footprints or any … *clues* as to who might have been here."

Finally he smiled. "You've just been dying to use that word, haven't you?"

I smiled sheepishly. "My entire life."

"And what's all this?" he said, gesturing to my coffee table.

"Dinner," I said. "Vinny's. You can have some … after we take a look outside."

"Oh my god. Is this *Rear Window*? Christ. I should have known," he said, shaking his head. "And the wine! We know what illusions a little red *vino* can put into your head, *rock-star extraordinaire*. To think I put my pants on for this."

Now it was my turn to glare. "I wouldn't necessarily call those pants, Lenny. I would call them loungewear. And no one asked you to put them on, Braveheart. I called to tell you that we must have struck a nerve somewhere with our questions. What other reason could there be for somebody to perpetrate such a crime?"

"Two more words you've been dying to use in the same sentence," Lenny mumbled. Still, he followed me through the house and to the back door. "Have you checked the trees for toilet paper? Everyone's hating that community service thing you're requiring for your final project, you know."

"Shh. Be quiet," I hissed as I silently shut the door.

"It's a little unheard of in a freshmen class," he hissed back.

I made a cutting motion at my throat and flipped on my flashlight. I could see nothing by way of footprints because the ground was dry and hard from the merciless wind that had been blowing lately. Besides, the narrow walkway that ran between Mrs. Gunderson's house and my own cut a path right down the middle of the backyard for any intruder who might want to escape undiscovered. Still, as I continued toward the garage, Lenny followed close behind me, glancing here and there at passing tree branches for hanging toilet paper.

I shone my flashlight as far as I could down the gravel alley in the direction the shape had travelled but saw only the yellow eyes of a cat staring back at me from the mass of azalea bushes that billowed out from another garage. In another instant, the eyes disappeared, and I shook my head. "Nothing here."

"Was the person on foot?" Lenny whispered.

I nodded. "I think so. I didn't hear a car, anyway." I flashed the light here and there as we made our way back toward the house, directing it in the tree once—just for fun. The back of the house had two entrances: the backdoor entrance, which I used all the time, and the back-porch entrance, which I rarely used. The back porch was small, a tiny square that in the evening grew too hot to sit in. Sometimes, though, in the morning, I would sit out there and drink my coffee, especially in the summer. During the school year, it was too cold, and I never had time.

I was beginning to open the backdoor when Lenny stopped me.

"Let's check the porch," he said.

"I don't know if it's open," I said as I reached for the door. It opened immediately when I tried it.

Lenny came in behind me, quietly pulling it shut. The screen door struck the rubber mat gently—once, twice—and I froze. Here was the *thud, thud* I had heard from the comfort of my living room couch.

Chapter Nineteen

"THAT'S IT. THAT'S the noise I heard. There actually was a person in my house," I said.

"Are you sure?"

I nodded. I felt too sick to speak.

"Come on. Let's get inside," said Lenny.

We walked into the house, and I grabbed ahold of the nearest kitchen chair. Lenny sat opposite me.

"This is about Austin, isn't it?" he said. "He *was* murdered."

I nodded again.

"I mean, I knew we knew, but I wasn't sure."

I hugged my knees to my chest.

"What if it was the murderer, Em? In your house—"

"Well of course it was the murderer. Who else would it be? I think we've ruled out my freshmen class," I said.

"Don't be flippant," said Lenny. "That's my thing. I'm serious here. Do you think we should call the police?"

"What would we tell them? That we've secretly been asking questions about Austin's death, and now his murderer is after me? You know it would all come out, and we just can't chance it. We must be close to something important."

Lenny didn't say anything, which meant he agreed.

"You're going to have to be careful, too, Lenny. Who knows? The murderer could be watching us right now."

Lenny jumped up and shoved his hands in his pockets. "Do you have a drink or something?"

"It's above the coffee maker."

He grabbed two short water glasses and poured us each half a glass of J&B. I could tell he was dazed, so I didn't say anything more. I just sat there turning my glass under the yellow light of the kitchen. Finally he took a drink and so did I.

"I don't think the murderer is watching us. And screw him if he is," said Lenny.

"Or her," I added.

"Or them," he said.

I raised my eyebrows. "I hadn't thought of that possibility." Adam and Jared in the back row came to mind, and just as instantly I dismissed them. Actually, I dismissed Adam, not Jared. Jared was mean enough to do something to Austin if he felt threatened. And who knows? Maybe there was someone else in the fraternity who felt the same way. It was a theory worth pursuing.

Lenny downed the rest of his drink. "Did you say something about Vinny's?"

I plopped the Styrofoam takeout box on the table. "Here. It's probably still warm."

He sat down in the chair and opened the box then looked at the empty glass in front of him.

"You're pushing your luck here," I said, taking the bottle and refilling his glass.

He shrugged his shoulders. "I know your state of confusion will be short-lived. I have to take advantage while I can."

"*My* state of confusion? *You* look positively bewildered." I finished my Scotch and put the glass in the sink. "Now let's go over what we have that could be of any importance."

"The gloves," Lenny said, his mouth full of food.

"The gloves. Right. We know Austin wasn't wearing them when he arrived at the coroner's office, and yet they are missing from the theater. There has to be something about those gloves that the murderer doesn't want found out." I grabbed one of the remaining breadsticks.

"Does that mean the murderer thinks you have the gloves?" asked Lenny.

"Maybe. But how could he be so careless?"

He took another swig of his drink. "Maybe something went awry, something unexpected."

"I suppose it's possible. If he doesn't have the gloves, he needs to find them before he's implicated. So he came here looking for them, or something else. He saw his chance while I was away getting my food; maybe he even knows my routine." I stood up. "I probably startled him when I returned, and he was still here. When I turned on the movie, he saw his chance to get away."

"It makes sense," Lenny said, rolling a long noodle around his fork, "except for one thing."

"Which is?" I prompted when he didn't immediately continue.

"Why would the murderer think you have the gloves? I was the one who called the coroner's office."

I walked back and forth across the kitchen. "That's a good question. I doubt the murderer even knows about the call to the coroner's office. He's probably just taking a stab in the dark. He knows Austin was my student, or he knows I have been asking questions about Austin's death."

"Or he knows you better than you think," added Lenny.

"True. It's dangerous to assume it's someone we don't know." I sat down at the table again. "We are going to have to be more careful, Lenny."

He shut the Styrofoam lid and pushed it away. "My lips are sealed."

Although his eyes were smiling, I knew he was worried. I

was, too. This was no longer just about Austin; I had to think of Lenny as well as my other associates. There was still a murderer on campus, and no one was safe until he was found.

Chapter Twenty

━━━

WHEN THE SUN rose the next morning, it divided the new October sky in two. On each side were dark gray clouds that threatened rain, and in between was an expanse of blue sky and the blazing sun. I imagined we were a lot like that, divided by dark and light. The person who had killed Austin, for instance, might have been a decent enough person. I didn't know anyone in town I'd consider inherently evil. Yet there was just enough darkness in that person to make him or her act unconscionably. Maybe it wasn't darkness so much as self-preservation. Human beings did inexplicable things when they felt threatened. That might have been the case here.

The sun tore away unexpectedly from the dark line of clouds, bursting into a complete circle of light. For a moment, the porch turned a brilliant white, and a desperate joy crept into my body. Then the moment was gone, and the porch turned dark again. I was left alone with my thoughts and fears. The murderer might have been in this very house—my house. But why? Obviously, he would have remained hidden had he wanted me dead, too. That thought didn't make me feel any safer. I stood up and decided to get busy and stay busy.

Anything else seemed too much like succumbing to fear and death.

A stack of student papers waited atop my dining room table, and I walked by them several times, sizing them up like an opponent. I had to be in the proper state of mind so as not to grade them too harshly or too leniently. I was preparing myself mentally by doing other chores: I washed my breakfast dishes, glanced through a photo album, and stroked my cat. All the while I was performing these tasks, one phrase Lenny had said last night kept repeating in my head: "something unexpected." Something unexpected had happened during the murder, and that something unexpected had to do with the gloves. I was certain of it. What I had to do was find that unexpected something or someone, and I had a good idea where to look. After searching our university intranet, I grabbed my coat and scarf and headed for the campus.

The hallways in Bodeman Hall were narrow and dark and smelled of musty furniture, and it took my eyes several minutes to adjust from the outdoor light. The Resident Assistant, or RA, said Sarah Sorenson was on the third floor, and I walked nearly to the end of the hall before I came upon her room. I knocked, but not surprisingly, no one answered. It being Saturday, the entire place was deserted except for a few kids who sat watching TV in the room downstairs. Disappointed, I started for the exit door. This time I took the fire escape stairs.

As the door clanged shut behind me, I saw Sarah getting into a little blue hatchback and called out to her. She looked up but did not recognize me, or seem to, as she continued to shove her duffle bag into her trunk. I ran down the steps to catch her, which wasn't easy considering my boot heels kept getting stuck in the metal holes that made up the stairs.

"Sarah!" I called out again, this time more urgently.

"Professor Prather?"

"Sarah, I wanted to talk to you about something. I can see you're on your way out, but this will just take a minute."

Sarah looked at her car. "Okay, but my parents are expecting me. I told them I was leaving right away."

"Is something wrong?" I asked.

"I … I don't feel well. I'm going home for the weekend."

She didn't look well, either. She was pale, and her normally shiny hair appeared unkempt.

"Listen, Sarah, I wouldn't ask you this unless it was important—and it involves you. You said that you were supposed to meet Austin on Saturday but that you never did. Are you sure about that?" She immediately bristled. I added, "The reason I ask is because I think Austin was in danger, and I think you might be too."

Her shoulders slumped forward slightly, and she stared at the ground.

"You see why this is important now?"

She looked up, and I saw tears in her eyes. She nodded.

"I think someone is following me, Professor Prather. I think they think I killed Austin, but I didn't!"

"Of course you didn't. Why would they think that?"

She dabbed at her nose with her sleeve. "I went to see Austin on Saturday, just like I said I would. I was a few minutes early, and he was sick. He said he had a headache, but I swear to God, I didn't know he was going to die! I didn't do anything to him. He said he was going to go back to the dorms and take a shower."

"A headache," I said. This meant someone got to him before Sarah did. Perhaps that someone was even still there. "What time did you get there?"

"Everybody was long gone. It must have been about six thirty when I left work."

"Where do you work?" I asked.

"Dynasty. "

Dynasty. I recalled the fight the young man had there and immediately wondered if it was her boyfriend. Claudia had said he was Asian, and it would explain her working there.

"Did Austin say why he was sick? Or was anyone with him?"

"No one was there. Just him. He said the paint thinner made him dizzy, and he was anxious to go back and take a shower. I could tell. That's why I stayed only for a few minutes. He was working on some furniture—a table." Tears began to trickle down her cheeks again, and she brushed them away with her sweater.

"This is important, Sarah, so think carefully. Was he wearing gloves when you saw him?"

She sniffed. "What kind of gloves?"

"Oh, you know, the rubber kind. The kind you might use with stain or paint." I was becoming impatient.

"I don't know. I don't know. How should I know?"

"Just try and remember. For Austin's sake," I added.

She closed her eyes, and put her fingers to her temples. She was an actress and a fine one at that. She had to be allowed her dramatics. Finally, she opened her eyes.

"Yes, he was wearing gloves. He was."

I knew it. I knew that before the police ever got there, someone had removed the gloves and perhaps the only piece of evidence that would link him or her to the murder.

"He was wearing gloves," Sarah repeated, more slowly now. "They should have protected him, right? Why didn't they protect him?"

"I don't know," I said. "I wish I did." I leaned in a bit closer. "Sarah, when I first came up, you said you thought someone was following you. What makes you think that?"

She looked around the parking lot before she answered. "Last night when I got back to my room, there was a note stuck in my door that said, 'I know about Austin. Meet me at the Tech Lab at nine o'clock.' I thought maybe it was my boyfriend." She rolled her eyes. "It looked like his handwriting, but it's hard to say. I don't see his handwriting that much because he usually texts. He gets weird ideas in his head about all my friends. I went and I waited until ten, when they close on Fridays, and walked back to the dorms. I felt like someone was watching me the whole time. When I got back to my room, stuff had been moved around and not been put back in exactly the same spot."

"What about your roommate? She must have seen something?"

She shook her head. "No, she leaves Friday right after her afternoon class to visit her boyfriend. He goes to State."

"What about the RA? Was she downstairs?"

Sarah smiled briefly. "She usually doesn't show up until curfew."

I could think of no more possibilities. I believed her. Someone had been in Sarah's place same as they'd been in mine. The person who killed Austin knew this campus, knew its habits and customs. He knew the dorms would be empty just as he knew I would be out getting my takeout from Vinny's … just as he knew the perfect place for a murder.

"Do you still have the note?"

She shook her head. "I shredded it at the Tech Lab. I didn't want anyone to see it. You believe me, don't you, Professor Prather?"

"Of course I do, Sarah. And I don't want to see any harm come to you … or anyone else. I'm glad you're going to your parents' house. It's the safest place for you. Before you go, though, I have to ask you one final question."

She released the handle to the car door, waiting.

"Austin was at a party Friday night for his fraternity. Did you pick him up?"

She shook her head. "No. I swear. I wasn't with him."

"But one of the guys said he left with a woman."

She shook her head again. "It wasn't me. I was with my boyfriend. You can ask him."

I could feel my brow furrowing. "Do you know if Austin had a girlfriend?"

"He had someone. A girl. I don't know if she was his

girlfriend, but I heard him talking to her on the phone."

"Were they serious?"

She crossed her arms. "*He* seemed serious. I never met her. I don't think she lived on campus."

"Did he ever say her name?" I pressed.

"No, not that I remember. We didn't talk about our significant others, if you know what I mean."

I nodded. I could imagine why the topic was off limits.

She pulled open her car door.

"Do you think someone did something to Austin?" she asked. "Is that why you're asking all these questions?"

I knew my own suppositions would give the girl no peace of mind, but I didn't want her to come to any harm either. "I think you need to be very careful until the police sort this thing out. If someone did do something to Austin, he or she might still be on campus, so don't go anywhere by yourself, especially at night."

She nodded, and I slammed the door shut. She drove away, leaving me alone in the parking lot. Only the trees made sounds, their brown leaves blowing violently back and forth in the wind. Sometimes I wondered how they could hang on in all that tumult.

As I walked toward Harriman Hall, I thought about what Sarah had said. Austin had been wearing gloves when she arrived, early and unannounced. This could have accounted for the something unexpected that the murderer did not anticipate. Startled, the murderer had to get out of there, leaving a piece of the evidence behind. Now the murderer was desperate to get that item of evidence back and was going to the people closest to Austin to find it. But who was close to Austin besides Sarah? Who was this mystery woman she had mentioned?

I stopped at the vending machine, pushed B5—Twizzlers—and started up the stairs. I had never been to a fraternity in my life, but I had no other move to consider. I had to invent a reason for going to one now. But what?

My office was cold, and I threw the sweater that was on my chair over my shoulders. When I opened the shade, a stream of sunlight flickered on and off as if it couldn't decide whether to stay or go. I sat, entranced, eating my Twizzlers and hoping an idea would come to me. When the candy was gone and no ideas had formed, I picked up *A Restless Heart*, a fairly well-formed romance novel about a woman who could not find her place in eighteenth-century London. I could completely relate. The picture was so dreamy and the plot so predictable that I found myself happily nodding off here and there among the pages. I was exhausted from not having slept the night before.

It wasn't long before I found myself in a drawing room with a man named Drake, bantering with the kind of witty wordplay I could never muster up in real life. Of course this was all a prelude to his cornering me near the bookshelf, where we happened to grab for the same book. Once our hands touched, a kiss was inevitable, and his smooth lips were the last thing I remembered as I was jostled awake by a man's voice.

"Really, Emmeline!"

It was Giles. Straightening up in my chair, I squawked, "Yes?"

He brushed off his coat sleeves. "I thought you were having a nightmare, but it's apparent that you were only under the spell of one of those *romance* novels."

I put the book, which had fallen to the floor, onto my desk and cleared my throat. "It isn't so much a romance novel as an in-depth study of eighteenth-century mores."

He crinkled his brow. "Let me guess. Drake is the one who is helping the young damsel defy those mores."

"You've read it, haven't you?"

"I don't have to. Your moans were testament enough to its … pleasures."

I felt my cheeks grow warm, but I could think of nothing to say.

Now a broad smile covered his face, and he looked around the room curiously. "What brings you in on a Saturday, anyway?

Your neighbor, Mrs. Gunderson? You look exhausted."

"I am. I was up half the night," I said.

"That woman is an absolute menace."

I shook my head. "She is, but it wasn't her."

"Ah! I know," he said, clapping his hands. "You were up all night grading papers."

"I did grade papers," I said, which was sort of true. The essay on top was a C. I could tell right away from the run-on sentences.

Now he became more serious. "You're still thinking about Austin. You know, Emmeline, there are services available on campus. Grief counseling. It may not be a bad idea to talk to somebody."

Giles knew there was more to my odd behavior than I was telling him, and he suspected grief was to blame. I needed him to continue to believe this so he wouldn't get involved. "I think you're right. I need ideas on how to move on."

"Yes," he said. "Moving on can be difficult, especially when we don't have explanations. But it is best. For now. We *will* find out what happened. In time. But who can say what that time will be?" He shook his head. "Honestly, I don't think Officer Beamer had a clue."

But he did have a clue; I was certain of it. He was just holding his cards very close to his chest.

"Anyway, if you need anything—I mean, *besides* the embrace of a devilish rogue—please let me know. I'm sure I can help you."

I smiled. "I do know that, Giles. Thank you."

As soon as he was gone, I turned to my computer and typed in the name of the fraternity where Austin had been a pledge. Their house was the grand old brick two story on Oak Street. I knew it well, and so did generations of men who oftentimes followed in their fathers' footsteps. While the website dropped words like "honor" and "excellence" and the house itself emanated tradition, I could see from the photos that partying and roughhousing were probably the major pastimes. Jared did take his leadership role in the fraternity seriously, though. Seriously enough to kill Austin? That was what I needed to find out.

Chapter Twenty-One

I RETURNED HOME from my office with renewed energy in my step. I wasn't good at lying, but I could stretch the truth with no problem. As I jumped into my '69 Mustang, a calculated decision to win the boys' approval, I put the finishing touches on my story. Although simple, it had taken a good deal of time to think up.

Two of the boys were in my class; they knew me. There was no avoiding this fact, so I decided to use their connection to my class to question Jared's whereabouts last night, which might tell me if he had been the one in my house. As I squealed my wheels into a parallel park, a skill I was proud of and drew attention to whenever possible, I rehearsed what I would tell Jared. I would tell him I had spilled coffee on his essay and would he be so good as to print me a copy. I had spilled plenty of beverages on plenty of papers. I had always haphazardly dabbed at them with paper towels and hoped it would suffice. But this time, no. I would tell him that the coffee had smeared the ink to the point that I couldn't read it. It was a minor lie that would garner only a small amount of humiliation. I killed the engine.

I walked up to the front door and knocked casually. It was one o'clock on a Saturday afternoon, a time you'd expect someone to be home at a large fraternity house. But I stood there for a good long minute before I knocked again, this time more forcefully.

Finally, a lady in her mid-fifties answered. Her hair was brown and curly and pulled back with a headband. She was busily turning pages in a calendar. "I'm sorry," she said, still focused on her work. "May I help you?"

"Hello," I said. "I'm looking for Jared. Is he here?"

Now she looked up and smiled sweetly.

"I'm his English teacher," I said.

She nodded doubtfully, and I debated whether or not I should rattle off the definition of a dangling participle.

"I teach at the university," I said. "He's in my class. I've spilled something on his paper, unfortunately, and need another copy."

"Of course you do, dear. I completely understand." She motioned to a sitting room at her right. "You sit here, and I will just go and fetch him for you."

"Thank you," I said, admiring the combination of oak and leather. From the dusty books and the polished floor free of scuff marks, I gathered that this room wasn't used much. On the walls were pictures of past houses, dating all the way back to 1910. I found myself smiling at the sophisticated-looking gentlemen with their jackets and hats, collars and ties. They all seemed so self-important, so ready to take on the world. Even the men in the more modern houses struck dignified poses, I saw as I progressed toward the current body of students. But then I stopped and looked again as I recognized some of the faces. Who would have thought some of our very own faculty had once been hormonal frat boys?

"Professor?"

"Hello, Jared. What a nice place this is."

He didn't sit down. Instead, he just stood there, confused.

"I suppose you wonder what I'm doing here, and really, it's

rather embarrassing. I was grading papers, see, and happened to spill coffee on yours." I waved my hands. "Completely illegible. Can't read a word of it."

He squinted at me. "So you want another paper?"

"I know it's rather ... unconventional, but I did want to hand back your paper with all the others. You know how I abhor lateness," I added, sounding rather like a schoolmarm. If only the housemother could hear me now. "I thought you could zip off a copy on the printer for me."

"I suppose I could do that." He looked around the room as if he could pull it from thin air. "I have it on my jump drive. *Shoot.* Just a sec." He bolted out of the room, leaving me with no opportunity to follow him. Instead I looked out the window.

Two boys putting on their jackets in the hallway looked in the room as they were passing, and I took it as an opportunity to speak. "Hi."

"Hey," they said in unison.

"I'm waiting for Jared," I said. "Do you guys live here?"

The redheaded boy with freckles laughed. "Do you want to see our ID cards?"

I laughed as well, trying to appear at ease. Really, though, I had no idea how the whole fraternity thing worked. For all I knew, they had ID cards. "You must have known Austin then, huh? Too bad about him. Jeez. It's all over the news." I tried to sound young. Perhaps I could even pass for a grad student.

"Austin was a cool dude," Freckles said. "I don't care what anybody else said. Farm kid or not, he had style."

"I wouldn't say style, I'd say determination," added the brown-headed boy wearing an expensive leather jacket. "Nothing was going to stop him from getting into the fraternity."

Jared broke up our conversation with his entrance, paper in hand. "Hey."

"Hey. We were just talking about your favorite person," said the boy in leather.

"Yeah? Who's that?" He handed me the paper.

"Austin," he said.

"You didn't like Austin?" I asked innocently.

The two boys laughed. "If the shoe fits," said Freckles.

Jared shoved his hands in his pockets, clearly irritated. "I liked him fine. I was the one who gave him the bid, idiot. I just didn't know if he'd make a good addition to the house."

"I think he would have," said the boy in the leather jacket. "He would have brought something different."

Freckles shoved him in a playful manner. "What? Like a pickup truck?"

"Did you need something else, *Professor* Prather?" said Jared, purposefully changing the topic.

This was underscored for the boys' benefit, and Freckles exclaimed, "Oh!"

"No, that will be all. I'm so sorry about the first copy. You know the story: late nights, early mornings. I'm sure you boys can sympathize." But the two students were already fighting for first dibs on the door handle.

"Goodbye, Professor," one mumbled, I'm not sure which, as they hurried out the door. I followed close behind.

"Oh I was going to ask you ..." I said, reopening the door.

Jared looked wary.

"Did I see you at Vinny's last night with ... Miriam?" Why that name fell out of my mouth instead of Jennifer or Rebecca, I had no idea. Maybe the Catholic Daughters were rubbing off on me. "She was in my literature class last year."

"Miriam? I don't know any Miriam," he said.

"Huh. I could swear I saw you there about eight o'clock ...."

He shook his head. "The game was last night."

He might as well as added "duh" to the end of his statement.

"Oh right. Of course, *the game*," I said, although I had no idea what game he was talking about. "That couldn't have been you. Well, thanks again for the re-print. See you in class next week."

He shut the door behind me.

Walking back to my car, I decided Jared had nothing to do with Austin's death. I was certain the person at my house was the person who had committed the murder. The two had to be connected. And if Jared had been my intruder, he would have looked guilty somehow or at least more suspicious of my presence.

Running the facts over and over again in my mind, I drove all the way down Main until I ran out of street and veered onto the highway. I stepped hard on the gas, snaking around the bluff, watching the town disappear behind me. Here was another nice thing about living on the prairie. You could get into your car and *drive*. There was no traffic. No stoplights. Only the dirt and sky, and if neither one bothered you much, you could drive as far as you wanted or needed to go without ever running out of road.

Something the fraternity boy had said kept replaying in my head: Austin wasn't the type to back down. I had to agree with the boy's assessment. Austin was probably polite and easygoing just up until the moment he wasn't. I had a feeling he would have gone along with the farm-kid stereotype right up until the second he punched somebody in the face for it. Maybe Jared was that someone. Maybe it was one of the other fraternity boys. Whoever it was, I needed to find him and soon.

Even if I had an idea of where to investigate next, I wasn't sure anyone would be there. There was something inherently lazy about a college town on a Saturday afternoon. Nobody did any work that didn't have to be handed in the next morning. And the truth was I didn't know who else had a complaint with Austin other than the fraternity boys. Of course there was one boy I suspected had a problem with Austin, and that was Sarah's boyfriend, Sean Chan. Sarah had admitted he didn't like boys calling or texting her. If that were the case, what had he possibly thought of Austin taking Sarah to a poetry reading or working with her at the theater? In fact, it was entirely possible that Sean followed Sarah after work that day all the way to the theater, sneaked in undetected, and saw something he wished he hadn't. I pulled off at the next dirt road and turned around. It was a great night for Chinese. Now I just needed to find a date, one who wouldn't mind analyzing the situation after the food was finished.

Chapter Twenty-Two

"So, ARE YOU asking me out on a date?" Lenny teased.

I fell onto my couch. "I told you, it's not a date. It's dinner. I was there all by myself a few nights ago. I don't want to draw undue attention by going there alone again. In fact, I think you kind of owe me a meal after scarfing down all my food from Vinny's."

"So now you're asking me out on a date *and* you want me to pay? Is that how you feminists roll these days?"

"Pretty much," I said. "Do you want to go or not?"

"Do I have to wear a tie?"

"Would you wear one if I said 'yes'?"

Lenny was silent for a few minutes. "That's a good question. Okay. I'll pick you up at seven."

"Seven. I'll see you then." I clicked off the phone, smiling to myself. I looked over at the stack of folders on my coffee table, and my smile slackened. I had five hours and not one excuse. I picked up my colored highlighters and went to work.

I took my students' writing seriously. I couldn't fly through a stack of papers as quickly as one of the teaching assistants. They had been taught to use egg timers and give each paper fifteen minutes, max. I had been taught that, too, but somewhere in between teaching assistant and professor, I began to add minutes to each paper, not take them away. If I couldn't give them my full attention, then they would get none at all. That was my personal teaching philosophy.

With a plan in my head for this evening, I worked through several papers, remaining completely focused on the students' individual needs and tailoring my feedback accordingly. Before nightfall, the stack of papers had shrunk considerably, and I felt a renewed sense of purpose that came from the tangible task of taking from pile A and putting into pile B.

"You're not wearing a tie," I said as I opened my door.

"You didn't ask me to," said Lenny.

I smiled and grabbed my purse. He still looked nice. He wore a dark gray shirt and a casual black blazer. His hair was damp as if he had just showered. I was glad I had put on my red A-line dress.

"After you," he said, holding the door.

The night had grown cold and windy, and I was happy my trench coat hung on the hook in the front porch. I shrugged into it, with Lenny's help, and tied the belt tightly around my waist. My black heels sunk into the grass as I crossed the boulevard and climbed into the passenger's side of Lenny's old Taurus, which smelled faintly of spearmint gum.

"So what's the plan?" he said, starting the car. "Do we know for sure Sean works there?"

I shook my head. "Not for certain. It's just a feeling I got the other night. I saw these two people fighting and wondered if Sean was one of them. I thought I heard 'Sean' in their conversation, but it was hard to tell with all that rapid-fire Chinese. He was the right age, good-looking, Asian—and Sarah works there. It has to be him."

"If you've never seen the kid, and I've never seen the kid, then how are we going to know it *is* the kid?"

I dismissed his question with the wave of my hand. "Nametags. Besides, it's never busy in there. Nobody can afford it."

He nodded, but I could tell he wasn't convinced. "So assuming he is wearing a nametag, and he is our waiter, and we do hold him hostage at the table for a few minutes, what are we going to say to him? How's the Crab Rangoon? By the way, where were you the day Austin Oliver was killed—or better yet, last night when Em's house was broken into?"

I threw him a look. "These things have to been done delicately, Lenny. You know that. We need to find an approach, a way in."

He shook his head. "A way in …. Well, there's Sarah … and Claudia, Sarah's teacher."

"Speaking of Claudia, you should have heard the way she assailed me on Friday. She even hinted I might lose my job."

"That's going too far, even for Claudia."

I nodded vigorously. "That's *exactly* what I said."

Lenny drove around the block, looking for an open parking space. He found one near the corner of the building. "So Sarah then. What do you know about her?"

He shut off the car.

"I know someone was in her dorm room last night and that she left for her parents' house this morning. I also know that she *did* meet Austin at the theater Saturday afternoon and that at that time he was wearing the gloves. He had a headache."

"Why didn't you tell me that on the phone? That's *news*. Did you believe her?"

I shrugged my shoulders. "About as much as I believe anyone these days."

"Which is saying 'every word,' right?"

I punched his arm.

"So let's think about this," he said, turning serious. "How are you and Sarah linked? Why your house and her dorm room?"

I shook my head. "I don't know. The murderer must think

that we were closer to Austin than we actually were."

"Speak for yourself. We know Sarah had a thing for him."

I did not argue. "She most certainly had something for him," I said. "And what's more, I think that if this Sean found out, it would mean trouble for Sarah. If it's the kid from the other night, he's a real hothead."

Lenny pulled open his car door. "Oh boy. There's nothing more enjoyable than an eighteen-year-old hothead."

As we walked into Dynasty, we were greeted by a very efficient—and very short—hostess. She smiled, took two menus from the rack beside the podium, and stalked off in the direction of the nearest booth. "Okay?" she asked.

"This is fine, thank you," I said.

A young boy appeared out of nowhere and filled our water glasses.

"Is Sean working tonight?" I asked with exaggerated politeness. The boy gave me a nod and walked away.

Lenny raised his eyes from his menu.

"See?" I said.

He nodded. "Do they have anything to drink here—besides beer and wine?"

"Sorry. It looks like you'll be drinking wine with me."

He closed his menu. "Wine with you is better than bourbon with anyone else."

"You already know what you're having?"

"Yeah, the beef and broccoli. It's what I always have."

I was puzzled. "But they have some really good food here. The Dim Sum is out of sight."

"No way. It's chicken or beef for me, Prather. Do you know what they put in those *authentic* dishes?"

I raised my hand, palm up, signaling for him to stop. "I concede the point."

"I can get you a shot of sake though," he said.

"A nice wine will do," I said, closing my menu.

The young man from the other night was making his way toward our table. It had to be Sean.

"Hello," he said. He was dressed in a crisply ironed white shirt and black pants.

Lenny looked at his nametag and then at him. "Hello, Sean."

He put his order form in his apron pocket. "I'm sorry, I can't remember you. My brother said you were asking for me. Are you the chemistry professor I was supposed to talk to about an internship?"

"Chemistry? No no. I'm in the English Department," said Lenny.

"Oh," was all Sean managed to say. He started to fumble for his pen.

"We know Sarah," I quickly added.

"Oh yeah. Sarah's an English major," he said, seeming to accept this explanation.

"Is she working tonight?" Lenny said, glancing around at nearby tables.

"No. She left to go to her parents' house." He sounded disappointed.

"That's too bad," I said. "I bet you wish you could have gone with her for the weekend."

He rolled his eyes. "Are you kidding? I'm here night and day. My parents own this place."

"I bet you had to work last night, too," said Lenny.

I smiled inside. He could be very clever when he wanted to be.

"Of course. Where else would I be on a Friday or Saturday night? They're our two busiest days of the week." Now he pulled out his order form and waited.

Lenny ordered a fine bottle of Malbec and Mandarin dumplings for an appetizer. Sean disappeared with the order.

"Sounds like Sean's a little bit disgruntled," said Lenny, taking a glug from his water glass.

I leaned in closer. "Who wouldn't be, especially with your girlfriend attending poetry readings and everything else with another guy?"

"But he said he was working last night. How could he have been at your house at eight?"

"True," I said. I sat back in the booth. Sean was coming with our wine.

Sean poured a splash of wine into Lenny's glass, and Lenny tasted and approved. Sean continued to fill Lenny's glass and mine. "You must be an English professor, too," he said to me.

I nodded.

"I think Sarah's mentioned you. You must teach her creative writing class," he said.

"No, I don't teach creative writing, but I did have Austin Oliver in my class. Did you know him?"

He put the bottle on the table. "He was more Sarah's friend than mine. He was always hanging around the theater. I guess he didn't have a real job. Lucky guy … well, maybe not so lucky after all."

The short woman cried "Sean!" from the kitchen. "Order!"

He hurried off, returning with the dumplings. "You guys ready to order?"

We gave him our orders, and he darted off before we could resume our questions.

Lenny raised his glass. "To Saturdays."

"To Saturdays."

"How'd those papers go for you? You get any of them done?" Lenny asked.

"Some. Quite a few." I was watching Sean's mom argue with him from behind the small window in the kitchen. "That woman is relentless."

Lenny took a big bite of dumpling and nodded. "The hand that rocks the cradle rules the world."

"Well, he looks like she's rocked his cradle one too many times. I wouldn't be surprised if he stalked out of here again tonight. He left on bad terms the other night, you know."

"I just hope he brings us our food first," Lenny said.

I laughed. "I just hope we can bring up Austin again without it being awkward."

Lenny raised one eyebrow. "It was awkward the first time."

"No way. I transitioned it in there nicely."

Lenny groaned. "Remember how I told you not to confuse people with paragraphs? You're doing it right now."

"But we don't know anything yet," I said.

"Yes we do. We know he wasn't at your house last night, and we know that this place has a decent and affordable wine list."

"Well that's true." I raised my glass again. "To affordability."

"May it not cost us our fortune," said Lenny with a clink of my glass.

"Besides," Lenny added, "if he were the intruder, he would have recognized you."

"True," I said with a sigh.

The immediate problems of Austin and Sean and Sarah started to recede from my brain as Lenny and I began to talk and eat and drink. The dumplings were delicious, and Lenny was right about the wine. It was very drinkable. I told him all about the fraternity fiasco. I suspected he deduced that I hadn't played it quite as coy as I would have liked. But I emphasized that I'd found out what I came for: Jared claimed he was at the game last night. And if we were sure the murderer and the housebreaker were one and the same, then Jared couldn't be the murderer.

When I finished my story, Lenny picked up the wine bottle and realized it was empty.

"Hey, where's the food? Shouldn't it be here by now?"

I scanned the room for Sean; I didn't see him. "Where's Sean?"

"If I knew that, I'd wrangle our food out of him."

"Excuse me, ma'am?" I said to a passing waitress with a blue-black ponytail. "Is our food on its way? Our waiter seems to have forgotten us."

"So sorry. Be right back." She walked quickly toward the kitchen. Within seconds, she reappeared with our food.

"Thank you," I said, "but what happened to Sean?"

"He was finished for the night. Enjoy." With that, she was gone.

Lenny and I looked at each other.

"Well that's odd," he said.

"Do you suppose we scared him off?" I said.

He placed his napkin on his lap. "Maybe, but I don't think so. I think Mommy Dearest did that all by herself."

"Maybe it was our talk of Austin?" I said.

He shrugged. "It could have been."

I picked at my food with my chopsticks, trying to trap a rogue noodle.

"You can't use those, can you?" he said.

"Not a bit."

"Good," he said, unwrapping his silverware. "I'm starving."

Chapter Twenty-Three

MONDAY MORNING CAME faster than I expected, especially since I had stayed up half the night grading the rest of my papers. I felt like one of my students pulling an all-nighter. Yet when I looked at the clock and it was well after midnight, I figured I might as well get up and finish the handful of papers I had yet to grade. I didn't regret my decision, and neither would Giles, but the face staring back at me from the mirror did. I dabbed extra concealer over my dark circles and applied a little more blush to my cheekbones. After fussing with my makeup, I didn't feel like fussing with my clothes, so I grabbed a long skirt and sweater from my closet, clipping my hair up into a messy bun. I threw the papers into a large canvas bag and walked out the door, coffee tumbler in hand.

Class went by quickly, and as soon as I'd handed back the last paper, I made for the door. I'd decided during class that I needed to go back to the theater. There was something sophisticated about the murder, a complexity devised with the help of experience and age—not youth. Now I wondered if the murderer were not a student but a person in authority, a person like Alex. This would explain the murderer's knowledge of my whereabouts Friday evening. Faculty members on a small campus such as ours knew just about everything about everyone else—even in other departments. For instance, the School of Arts and Sciences loved to criticize the popular Business School. It stored rumors about it as a homemaker might store raspberry jam. Especially when enrollment was down, we'd pull out our winter fodder, which helped us feel safe from budget cuts and all other threats aimed at anything old or artistic. English just happened to fall into both categories.

I swerved between groups of students and teachers and laptop carts, silently cursing their immobility. I didn't see people but obstacles in my way, so when André tapped my shoulder, I jumped noticeably, despite the fact that the hallway was buzzing with traffic.

"Emmeline! I'm so sorry. I didn't mean to startle you," he said.

"You didn't," I lied. "How are you?"

A smile spread across his face. "I am walking on water."

"Should I call the pope?"

"You should call anyone you like and tell them that you and I are headed to Paris this spring." He squeezed my shoulder in a feeble embrace.

I stood baffled for a few moments, puzzling over his words or his touch—I wasn't sure which. Then it hit me. "Of course! The grant. You got the money."

"Correction. The *French* Department got the money."

His radiant smile made it impossible for me to grasp the ramifications of his statement. "We don't have a French Department," I finally said.

"Dean Richardson says if I can sustain enrollment this spring, he will put the idea to the test this fall. And I'm happy to say that you will be my first new hire."

I just stood there, perplexed, and for some absurd reason I found myself thinking about Lenny.

"No more freshman composition … yay!" He did a little cheer and waved his hands around.

"This is terrific news, André," I said. "I am so happy for you."

"And you, Em. I am so happy for *you*." He took my hands and grasped them for a moment before releasing them. "You are happy at this news, no?"

I smiled. "Of course. It's what I always wanted. I am ecstatic. Absolutely ecstatic. I just happen to be on my way to an appointment right now that I can't miss. I apologize."

"No, no. You go. I understand. We will talk about this later. Perhaps over dinner again?"

Was this André's way of asking me out on a real date? It was too much, and I had too many other things on my mind to think about at the moment. "Of course," I said, turning toward the exit. "Great … good. Can't wait. See you soon then."

Claudia was right, I thought as I shoved my empty coffee tumbler into my tote. This ordeal with Austin was making me positively strange. All my dreams were coming true three steps in the other direction, and here I was, walking away. It was as if I didn't care at all about the future, only the past and how it related to one person: Austin. I needed to find answers and put my preoccupation with his death to rest once and for all.

THERE'S SOMETHING EERIE about a theater not in use—its size, its curtains, its empty seats.

And then there was the murder; it had happened right here on this stage. An act of murder. It sent goose bumps all over me to think that Austin had lain inside this theater, dead, for hours in a campus of five thousand. How could that be? It couldn't possibly, and yet it had been. I closed my eyes for a moment and then opened them, shaking my head to rid myself of the tingly feeling slowly passing over my body. I flung open the door, disgusted with my own fears.

Luckily I caught the door—and myself—just in time before making a grander entrance than I intended, for there were two people rehearsing on stage. I stood silent for a moment beside the door, listening, before I realized I recognized the voices. One belonged to Alex; the other, I couldn't completely comprehend, but from the softness of it, it must have been Dan's. I inched slowly against the wall, toward the stage, and discovered it *was* Dan. And they certainly weren't rehearsing for the play.

"I explained to you already that nothing in my theater killed that student. She can look all she likes, but she isn't going to find one thing, not one," said Alex in loud voice. Obviously he wasn't worried about being overheard.

Dan's response was much quieter. "I'm just asking why Officer Barnes keeps coming around. Obviously she thinks *something* in here is responsible."

"Or do you mean some*one*, Dan? Isn't that what you're really implying? By all means, accuse me of killing the boy, but please do so in a direct manner. I can't take all this wishy-washy bullshit."

I clapped my hand over my mouth to keep my surprise from escaping.

"Come on, Alex. I didn't say that." Dan shoved his hands into his pockets.

"You didn't have to. You sulk every time I come around, looking at me out of the corner of your eye. And the set? It's weeks behind!"

"A few days at most … and I think that's pretty good with everything going on around here lately."

I was impressed with Dan's newfound nerve. At least his voice had lost its shakiness.

"Pretty good? Pretty good? When has pretty good ever been enough for you?" boomed Alex.

"It's always been enough for me. It's just never been enough for you," said Dan. "Nothing's ever good enough for you. And that's why … that's why I can't believe you weren't here the night Austin died. You live, eat, and breathe in this theater."

Alex just laughed. "There. You see? I knew you were holding something against me. I'm glad you finally had the gall to say it. Now maybe you'll be able to get some work done."

Dan remained motionless. "So? Were you?"

Alex stopped mid-stage, and the theater went as quiet as I'd ever heard it. I could feel my heart knocking in my chest as loudly as the narrator thought he heard the heart of the buried man in Poe's "Tell-Tale Heart." For a moment, I imagined I had been discovered. Then Alex turned to Dan.

"How dare you insinuate I had anything to do with that boy's death! No wonder the police keep hanging around here—feeding off your every word. I don't need to answer to you, and I won't. You, you … don't even have a PhD!"

With that, Alex stormed off the stage, and Dan muttered, "It always comes down to that."

Dan, like me, suspected that Alex knew more than he was letting on, but what it was exactly, I couldn't say. It wasn't as if he had a motive for killing Austin; he barely knew him. And as he told Dan the day of our meeting, it was nice to have a volunteer like Austin around. Did that mean he wouldn't cover up something to protect his precious theater? Not at all. I believed he would go to any lengths necessary for the show to go on as planned. The theater, after all, was his life.

Alex was here constantly. He didn't have a family or any close friends to care for at home, and in the midst of a production, he was prone to seven-day work weeks. He had said as much before to our committee and was proud of it. What if Dan were right, then, and Alex had been at the theater the night Austin was murdered? Perhaps there was something wrong with the gloves, something defective. That would explain why they were missing; it might also explain why Sophie kept "hanging around," as Dan put it. She didn't believe anyone would be dimwitted enough to bring the gloves to his or her own house, which would only underscore the person's guilt.

I waited for Dan to leave the stage, but he didn't. He looked ghostly, moving slowly and deliberately against the pale city streets. At any moment, I expected to hear the grim voice of Javert from *Les Mis*, but all was quiet and remained quiet, affording me no opportunity to leave or even move.

I don't know how long I stood like that—it felt like hours— but when Dan left, I finally squeezed open the door. The light pierced my eyes, and I had to blink the tears away before I could see. I reached into my purse for a tissue and was startled by a woman's voice.

"Em! What are you doing over here?"

Two women were mere inches away from me, waiting for an answer, but I was still disoriented and couldn't manage a word. Instead I dabbed at my eyes, recognizing in quick bursts that it was Ann, from Women's Studies, dressed in slim jeans and knee-high boots, and the long-fingered lady, draped in a fabulously yellow shirt. "Hi Ann. And … Martha? Right?"

"Right you are," said Martha. "Emmeline and I met the other day," she told Ann by way of explanation. "Ann just stopped by to go to lunch. The theater is a popular place today."

"Small world, right? You can join us if you're not busy. We'd love to hear your take on the new electronic grading system," said Ann. "It's cumbersome, if you ask me."

I was quite hungry, and Ann was always fun to talk to. Plus, I wanted to ask her about Owen's interview. But the thought of an hour-long lunch was unbearable because my mind was still on Alex and Dan's conversation. I would probably be less than adequate company. "Thanks, I'd love to, but I have so many papers to grade, I'd better not. I'm just going to grab a quick bite."

"That's okay. We'll do it another time. Hey, we didn't have a meeting with Alex, did we?" asked Ann, glancing around the entryway.

By the anxious look on her face, I could tell that she thought she had been left out of something. I did my best to reassure her she had not. "No, no. I just peeked in at the set to see what they came up with. Have you seen it? It's awe-inspiring. Your Art Department is doing a terrific job."

"It takes a village, doesn't it?" answered Martha. "I can't believe all the people Alex pulled into this production. Even Ann here," she said with a playful push. "It's going to be well worth it, though. Well worth the work."

"Indeed. Anything great always is. Let's just hope it opens on time and without a hitch. It would be a shame to waste all this talent."

"Why wouldn't it?" asked Martha.

Ann and I looked at each other. "You know," said Ann. "The accident."

Martha dismissed the suggestion with a wave of her hand. "If I know Alex, and I most certainly do, he won't let anything interfere with opening night. As they always say, 'The show must go on.' "

Ann began buttoning up her leather jacket. "I suppose you're right. It feels a little morbid just the same."

"I have to agree," I said. "It's going to be hard to forget Austin died right there as I'm watching the play."

"I suppose a lot of people will be thinking the same thing. Anyway," Martha said in an extra chipper voice, "we should think of it as a memorial, a tribute, to Austin in some way. After all, he himself was an active member of the theater."

I forced my jaw to remain steady. Some academics really had a flare for the dramatic. "Well, have a good lunch, ladies," I said. "It was nice seeing you again, Martha."

"You, too, Em," said Ann. "And stop by soon. We *need* to chat."

"I will. We have a lot to catch up on." I gave her a sly wink, and she smiled.

I was the first one out the door, and I rushed to the streetlight to cross. A cold October wind was blowing, and my eyes began to water all over again. Martha and Ann drove by in Ann's little Honda and gave me a beep. I waved back, wondering what they must think of me with tears sliding down my face.

After picking up a sandwich to go at the Express, I came across Claudia Swift as I was exiting the commons. She was discarding her lunch tray.

"Claudia!"

She turned and looked.

"How was your weekend?" I asked her as I approached.

"Wonderful."

"Wonderful?" That was it? When I asked Claudia a question, I never received a one-word answer.

She smiled. "Yes, wonderful. Gene and I have decided to take a couples' cruise in the spring. If everything goes as planned, he will propose to me in Italy."

I was confused. "But you're already married."

"Not really. Not anymore. We must renew our vows before I will allow him back upstairs."

My anticipation for spring semester was growing every day.

"Are you headed out?" I said.

"Yes. Let's walk."

"So I wanted to ask you something." I wrapped my long knit scarf twice around my neck.

"I could tell," she said, pulling on her leather gloves.

"Really? Okay. Well, it's about Thomas Cook."

"I know," said Claudia. "His marriage to Lydia seems highly suspect."

"Now that you mention it … but that's not what I was going to ask you."

She turned to look at me.

"It's his research," I said. "I thought his PhD was in composition and rhetoric, but the other day, he told me he was reading an article on temper and violence. What am I missing?"

"A lot. If you'd hang around after the faculty meetings, instead of darting out right away, you would have heard him talking about his new research project: violence on American campuses."

I raised my eyebrows as if surprised. "Wouldn't that research be better suited to a sociology professor or something?"

"Not the way he's looking at it. He's examining the *language* journalists use to portray violence on college campuses. He's very smart and very hip and very young. My bet is he won't stay in Copper Bluff long."

I threw up my hands, and my sandwich jumped inside the paper sack. "He's only a few years younger than I am."

"Well, it doesn't matter. He's married anyway."

"That's not why I was asking," I said, exasperated. "I was asking because he inquired about Austin Oliver. I had to know why."

She stopped and pointed her finger at me. "I won't participate in this witch hunt, Em. You and I both know it's become a substitute for your research. When's the last time you finished a chapter? Don't answer. I can see a lie forming on your lips. Now go. Stop thinking about Austin Oliver. Start thinking about Heloise. Write. Write as if your life depended on it." With a dramatic toss of her hair, she turned toward Harriman Hall.

I walked across the remainder of campus alone, but despite Claudia's advice, I did not stop thinking about Austin. At least I knew now that Thomas Cook's interest in Austin was academically related. After running into him at the theater, I had suspected he was there for a more sinister reason.

When I arrived home, I snuggled up on my couch with a cup of coffee. Then I called Lenny and told him what I had overheard in the theater.

"Why didn't you tell me? I would have met you there," he said.

"Because I want you to come back tonight with me."

I heard a deep sigh on the other end.

"Hold your air antics," I said. "I think Dan is on to something. Alex works incessantly on a production. How is it that he wasn't the one to find Austin? How is it that he remains clueless about Austin's death?"

"Okay, so let's just say that we mastermind our way into the theater undetected. What then? What are we looking for?"

I sat up straight, putting my coffee cup down hard on the table. "For starters, the missing gloves. And who knows? Maybe the poison that was used to kill him. I'd love to get a good look at that cleaning cabinet."

"I thought Sophie said it was poison, not Pine Sol."

Lenny could really be insufferable. "Well, we don't know what Alex is hiding in there until we look, do we? Besides, Pine Sol can be poisonous when it's ingested."

Now he laughed out loud. "Gloves, poison, a fake ID, and getaway cash? The sky's the limit when it comes to your imagination."

"So are you coming or not?" I said.

"Of course. What time?"

I looked out my window as if determining the time by the color of the sky. I knew the campus doors were locked at ten o'clock, so there was no way we were getting in there after hours without a key.

"Nine thirty? What do you think?" I asked.

"That's what I was thinking. Okay. I'll pick you up a little after nine," said Lenny.

"Meet me at my house. We'll walk over."

"Ah yes. Tire tracks."

I smiled. "And wear black."

"I was thinking camouflage …."

"You don't own anything camouflage. One of your Beatles t-shirts will do just fine."

"You know Prather, I've had just about enough of your apparel suggestions. You're starting to get downright … personal."

"Don't be late," I said, clicking off the phone. I gathered my legs beneath me, curling up in the corner of the couch. Last night's sleep had been fleeting at best, and tonight's would be even worse, for my mind had a hard time quitting an engagement even long after it had quit me. Dickinson jumped onto my lap, as if on cue, and began purring and shedding copiously. I knew there was no chance of my large cup of coffee taking its effect now, and my eyelids succumbed to the heaviness weighing them down. Ten minutes ... surely ten minutes never killed anybody.

I had read enough about dreams to be leery of them, to watch for unconscious signs of distress and despair. Every dream I had ever looked up in my dream dictionary was defined as an obstacle dream; I was always going through or about to go through or overcoming some sort of obstacle. I concurred with the book. Yes, life presented its share of obstacles, and I found myself constantly entangled in their courses. But this dream—this ten-minute interlude—I didn't dare to look up. For if it were truly a sign of my repressed feelings, I didn't know a thing about love or romance or all those things I had read about in books. It was incongruous, really. To think that I had arrived at this age so completely naïve.

I pushed the cat aside, blaming her for my hot cheeks. "Good god, Dickinson! Look at all this fur. No wonder I'm sweating." I took the lint roller off the coffee table and rolled it over my sweater. "You'd think you didn't bathe fifty times a day."

Dickinson sat looking right through me.

"Go on," I continued. "Sit and stare. You're not the borderline insomniac. You can't imagine the things one can dream when bereft of sleep. It means nothing. My dream about Lenny means nothing." I folded up my blanket. "Actually, it means one thing. It means I'm tired—exhausted. It means I can't even dream sanely anymore." I shook my head. "Imagine what I'm like conscious. A walking time bomb!" I tossed the pillows from the floor to the couch. "Well, that's all going to change when I figure out this thing tonight. You wait and see."

Dickinson was no longer listening. She had rearranged herself on the folded blanket, her back turned toward me.

Chapter Twenty-Four

I LOOKED OUT the front window—for the fourth time. *Damn Lenny.* He was late. It was almost nine thirty. Stalking into my office, I looked out the window and saw headlights from down the street; it had to be him. I put on my black windbreaker and wasn't disappointed. He pulled up in front of my house and shut off the engine. When he knocked on the door, I was just grabbing my mini-flashlight.

"Sorry," he said. "Mrs. Baker needed help with her cat. Damn thing climbed down the air exchange vent."

I could hardly scold him with that excuse. "The air exchange vent?"

He shrugged. "She's painting, so she took off all the vents—not a good idea. You should have seen her teetering up there on her ladder, ready to bust a hip. I told her I'd go over there tomorrow and help her finish up …. That is, if I'm still alive."

I tied my tennis shoes.

"I didn't know you owned athletic attire."

"Kickboxing phase," I explained.

"Ah," Lenny said. "I went through my own Tae Bo phase.

What was that guy's name? Billy Blanks? Got through the first CD."

"At least you still got the CD. All I got was sore knees from a little powerhouse named Candy."

"Who really names their kid Candy? It ought to be outlawed."

"I know," I said, grabbing my house key. "Come on, let's go."

It was dark, but the faint glow from the street lamps lighted our way to the campus. The breeze nearly howled through the tops of the old trees, and the shadows played tricks against the gray sky, making the street seem unfamiliar. The friendly old houses looked tall and sinister and the students shifty and dangerous. I looked at Lenny, handsome in his black jeans and jacket, and wondered if I was doing the right thing. I didn't mind about myself; I had to see this through. But Lenny? Would he have become entangled in something like this without me? And wasn't there a chance—a good chance—that this adventure was going to lead to more trouble?

"You know, Lenny, maybe it would be best if I go alone. I'm smaller than you are—"

"Don't grow a conscience now, Em. It's unbecoming. Besides, I'm a big boy. I can make my own decisions."

I opened my mouth then shut it. If I could be stubborn, he could be downright obstinate. I hesitated.

He glanced over at me and put his arm around my shoulders, giving me a quick squeeze. "Come on. This will be a breeze compared to your grammar final."

I smiled and walked a little more quickly, saving my doubts for later—two o'clock in the morning or thereabouts.

A few blocks more and we were on campus, cutting across the grounds toward the streetlight. Past the road, we could see the dark theater and didn't bother to wait for the light since traffic was minimal. Unlike every other building on the main campus, though, the theater had little cover from trees, so anyone might have seen us crossing the parking lot. Still, it didn't take us long to get to the side door, which was open.

The long hall was deserted and so were the offices. Thankfully the same art exhibit had been on display for the last three months. When the semester was in full swing, several budding artists would crowd the hall with their canvases and sculptures, and the building would see more traffic. But tonight, nothing but ominous silence awaited us.

"There's no way the basement door is unlocked. Let's start in the theater," I whispered.

Lenny nodded and followed silently behind me.

The door closed with a click that seemed to reverberate throughout the auditorium. I cringed, but Lenny didn't notice since it was so dark. There were no windows, no stray rays of light to illuminate our way. I looked around, hoping my eyes would adjust, but it was no use. Lenny began fumbling with his coat.

"Pen light," he whispered.

"Let's wait," I whispered back. "Just in case."

We crept along the wall until we got to the stage door. Instead of using it, we crawled up the side of the stage. I felt a little bit like Alice in Wonderland as I tiptoed onto the set.

"It doesn't look like anyone is here," I whispered.

"Let's hope not." He flicked on his light. It illuminated a small circle of white, which he flashed back and forth. "So where to?"

A kettle hung over a faux fire looked like a good place to hide evidence, and as I pointed to it, Lenny flashed his light inside. We found nothing except freshly painted metal.

"We're probably wasting our time," he whispered. "The cops had to have gone through this stuff already. Besides, who would hide the evidence at the scene of the crime?"

I fumbled for my own flashlight. "Someone smart, that's who. Then he wouldn't be implicated if it were found. He could blame it on any number of people."

"I'm going to check over here," said Lenny, walking toward a long rack of costumes. "Maybe the gloves were disguised as part of another costume. Be careful."

I nodded, staying close to the set of *Les Mis* since constructing set pieces had been Austin's area of expertise. In addition to the garden gate where Cosette and Marius would proclaim their love for each other, there was a fake brick wall with scaffolding, steps, and a ladder. It was amazing, really, all the work that had been done already with much more still required. Two grocery carts held building materials I assumed were still to be added, and various buckets and trays littered the stage.

"Hey, look," said Lenny, "gloves."

I quickly flashed my light in his direction. "What?"

He held up his arms, garbed in ladies' opera gloves.

"Cute," I said, walking in his direction. "Did you find any of the rubber variety?"

"Oh I always carry those in my back pocket."

"And how convenient, a bed," I said, pointing to what was probably Fantine's deathbed since it was small and narrow. Here Jean Valjean would make his promise to take care of her daughter, Cosette, for the rest of his days.

Lenny gasped audibly. "I'm shocked at the direction this conversation is taking. Maybe Giles was right. The stress—"

We heard the noise—a door opening backstage—at the same time, shut off our lights, and stood silent. Neither of us dared move as we heard footsteps coming toward us. Suddenly the footsteps stopped and retreated back toward the door.

I seized Lenny's hand and pulled him toward the bed, squishing in between the brick wall and the headboard. Seconds later, we heard the footsteps again and then the drone of the stage lights warming up. I stared at Lenny with an open mouth. With one quick walk across the stage, the person in the theater would know our location. Lenny pointed under the bed, and I mouthed the word "How?" He held up one finger and then began to slouch down. When he was lying on his back, he inched his way under the bed, and I followed suit. The entire time I could hear what sounded like men's dress shoes walking up and down the steps from the costume shop to the stage.

As I lay on my back, my chest heaved involuntarily, and I began to feel as if the bed were getting closer and closer to my face. A pulse hammered in my head, and I hoped Lenny didn't realize how close I was to jumping out of my skin. I kept imagining the person sitting down on the bed, sinking deep into the mattress and bedsprings, pinning me to the floor. Frozen and silent, I watched for the first sign of movement.

As I lay there examining the mattress, though, I began to think what an excellent hiding spot a bed was, and my breathing became more regular. It was the first place I ran to as a kid, hiding my mother's copies of *Modern Romances* magazine and piling blankets up over my lumpy form. A thought entered my head, and I instinctively looked at Lenny, but he was facing the other direction, presumably watching for the man's feet to appear.

When the footsteps faded again, I ever so slowly reached with my right hand until I felt the side of the mattress. Then I began searching between it and the dust ruffle. Nothing. I scooted lower, drawing my knees up so as not to expose my feet. Lenny touched my shoulder, but I couldn't possibly explain what I was doing. I reached my hand in again and made contact with something, but I couldn't be certain what because the footsteps were back again, this time for good. There were no more trips backstage. Instead, the person crawled up the ladder, onto the scaffolding, a long cord in tow.

Lenny pointed in the person's direction, and I nodded, acknowledging that I had indeed seen him—or at least the shoes, so I assumed it was a man. There was nothing we could do but wait. Suddenly I heard a click and then a male voice say, "Damn it!"

I recognized the voice as Alex's and was not surprised. I assumed he was the one working late. Still, I wished it had been Dan. Dan was less menacing than Alex, and if we had to be found out by anyone, he would have sympathized more with our situation. Just today Dan had been trying to find answers to Austin's death.

Now Alex began to climb back down the ladder, following the cord offstage.

I knew this was my only opportunity, and I boldly took it. I sat up as far as I could and grabbed wildly between the mattress and spring, hoping to find what I had imagined were the gloves. Lenny gripped my leg desperately, but I shooed him with my free hand. Unsuccessful in my half-hearted approach, I stuck my head out from beneath the bed and lifted up the mattress, seizing the rubbery material as I slid back under the bed.

I held it up to my face, squinting to examine it. Five fingers. Now ten. This had to be it—the gloves! I shoved them in Lenny's face, and he nodded. The footsteps were back, so I quietly folded the gloves over my chest, trying to curb my excitement. It was hard. The gloves were the first real piece of evidence that supported my theory as to what might have happened here Saturday night.

The cord clanged up the metal ladder again, step by step, but this time, when Alex reached the top, drilling followed. The noise startled both of us out of our silence. Luckily, the loud buzz covered up any commotion we may have made under the bed. The drill started and stopped several times, and I imagined Alex was drilling something into place. We lay trapped beneath the bed for what seemed like eternity, neither of us comfortable on the hardwood floor, the sound of the drill keeping us on edge. Finally, Alex came down the ladder, coiling the cord as he went. For several minutes, we didn't hear anything at all; still, the lights remained on. I turned toward Lenny, and he shrugged his shoulders. We waited then waited some more. Finally the lights shut off, and we were engulfed in darkness again, not daring to speak.

Slowly, I unzipped my jacket, sliding the gloves inside. I wondered if I was leaving my fingerprints all over the gloves or if fingerprints could stick to rubber. Then a terrible thought occurred to me: had I in fact ruined the evidence that would convict Austin's murderer? Too late now. If I returned them to their hiding place, the killer might come back for them, and then where would we be? I gingerly zipped up my jacket.

"Go?" The word was barely audible. I pointed to the exit with my thumb.

Lenny didn't respond but moved closer to the dust ruffle. I inched closer to him. We did this several times until we found ourselves out from beneath the bed. Creeping to the edge of the stage, we slid off, Lenny silently helping me down. Neither of us turned on our lights; instead, we blindly followed the length of the wall until we were at the door.

Now the hallway was pitch black, and I wondered how long we had been in there. Thankfully, the light from the street shone through the windows of the front doors, giving us enough light to make our way down the hall. We moved noiselessly toward the side door, keeping close to the wall. The lack of light reassured me that Alex was gone, but we would know for sure once we opened the door and could see the parking lot.

Lenny pressed down on the bar in the middle of the door, but despite his best efforts, it still made a loud noise. He waited for a moment and then pushed it open a crack. We scooted out, allowing it to close slowly behind us.

It took every ounce of self-restraint I had not to dash headlong across the parking lot, for now we were exposed under the bright outside lights. Instead, I followed Lenny, who briskly turned toward the sidewalk. I glanced behind my shoulder, looking for Alex's car, when I suddenly collided with Lenny's solid back.

"What the—" I began, then quit. I realized why Lenny had stopped.

"Ms. Prather, isn't it? I can't imagine what you're doing out so late—and on a school night, too."

It was Detective Beamer, and he had caught us in the act.

Chapter Twenty-Five

━━━

MY MOUTH WENT dry as I met Detective Beamer's accusing eyes. What could I possibly say that would explain our presence at the theater this time of night? I felt like one of my students, trying to come up with a plausible excuse as to why my paper was late.

"Detective Beamer. Hello. We were just leaving the theater."

"That much is obvious," said Beamer. "What were you doing in there?"

I glanced at Lenny; he had nothing for me. "Well you see, I'm on this committee. We meet about various artistic endeavors. Like the play *Les Miserables*? Hammer out all the particulars before the production."

Beamer crossed his arms. "You mean to tell me you were in a meeting? So why the catsuit?"

"No, no. I wasn't in a meeting *tonight*. Tonight I was simply helping Alex with some … drilling. This is what I wear when I do any sort of, you know, heavy labor."

"I think you both better come with me down to the station. Who is your friend here? Haven't we met before?"

I looked desperately toward Lenny. I didn't want him to get

into trouble. "Oh, he's not my friend. He's just—"

"I'm Lenny Jenkins," said Lenny, sticking out his hand.

"You're a professor, too?" asked Beamer.

Lenny nodded.

"English?"

Lenny nodded again.

"I remember now. You were with Ms. Prather the first time I was over here."

I could just imagine Giles's face when he heard we had been hauled down to the police station in the middle of the night. Perhaps even arrested for obstructing justice—or worse yet, murder! For all Beamer knew, *we* were the ones who had killed Austin and were erasing evidence we had left behind. It looked bad, indeed, for both of us. I had to do something fast to keep us from going down that road to prison.

"Look, Detective, I'm going to level with you. I wasn't drilling with Alex—"

His eyes turned mocking. "You're kidding."

"But he was here, and what's more, I've found something that might be very important to solving Austin's murder."

Lenny rubbed his forehead at the sound of the word.

"Murder?" said Beamer.

I looked around the parking lot and spotted what I assumed was his car. "Can we go somewhere where I can show you? Perhaps your car?"

Beamer looked from Lenny to me. For a moment, I thought he was deciding which of us to handcuff first. But then he pointed toward his car. "This way."

We walked in front of him all the way to his brown sedan.

He unlocked the door with the click of a button. "In the front, both of you."

Thankfully, it didn't have bucket seats. Still, the middle seat was uncomfortable at best, and I had a hard time locating the seatbelt.

Beamer slid into the driver's seat. "What are you doing?"

"I'm sorry, I don't see the strap—"

"Are we going somewhere?" he said.

Lenny shook his head.

"Well, yes," I said. "I'd like to gain some distance from the theater—just in case we're being watched. Would you mind going for a little drive?"

Beamer stared at me then glanced at Lenny. Lenny fastened his seatbelt.

"You know the problem with you academics?" said Beamer, starting the car. "You don't live in the real world. You live in some sort of fantasy land."

"We hear that a lot," I said as we turned out of the parking lot. "I suppose there's some truth in it, too."

Beamer pulled down a side street and turned off the lights. He left the car running. "So what's this evidence? Let me hear it."

"I can do better than that. I can let you *hold* it," I said. "But you have to promise that you won't take Lenny and me down to the station."

"I can't promise you anything until I see the evidence."

I unzipped my coat and gave him the gloves. "I found these stuffed underneath a mattress in the theater. I believe they're the ones Austin was wearing the day he was murdered."

Beamer turned them over carefully in his hands. "How would you know that? How would you know unless you had something to do with the murder?"

I let out the breath I didn't know I was holding. "So you *did* know about the gloves."

"Of course I knew about the gloves," said Beamer, his eyes narrowing into a glare.

"How?" asked Lenny.

"You first," said Beamer, grabbing a plastic bag from the side of his door.

"Dan said he was certain Austin was wearing gloves because they were missing from the theater," I explained.

He raised his eyebrows. "And how did you know we didn't already have them?"

I looked at Lenny, then back at Beamer. I didn't want to admit to our call to the coroner. "You and Sophie kept coming around, looking for a piece of clothing."

This explanation must have seemed plausible to Beamer because he didn't ask any more questions. I continued. "I, like you, wondered if they might be stashed somewhere in the theater, so tonight, when everybody left, Lenny and I went in to take a look. Little did we know that Alex, the work-a-maniac, would be hard at it."

Beamer put the gloves in the bag and zipped it shut. He took out a package of Handi Wipes, wiped his own hands carefully and gave us each one as well. "And what did Alex say when he saw you?"

"Nothing. He didn't see us," said Lenny, wiping his hands. I did the same.

"How can we be sure he wasn't there the night of Austin's *death*?" I asked, choosing my words more carefully. "Isn't this proof that he could have been working late that night as well?"

From the skeptical look on Beamer's face, I thought for certain he would criticize my line of reasoning. Instead he put the car into drive. "It's coincidental; that's for sure."

Lenny and I looked at each other as he pulled away from the curb.

"Where are you taking us? The station?" I said, unable to keep the anxiety out of my voice.

He shook his head. He approached the stoplight and took a left, then a right. We were driving past the main campus, which looked friendly and bright again from the comfort of the detective's car.

"Hey, this is my street ... this is my house." I looked at Beamer, puzzled, as he pulled in behind Lenny's car. He put his car in park.

"I know it's your house, Ms. Prather. I know it's your house because a few nights ago your neighbor, Mrs. Gunderson, called 911, stating that she had seen a suspicious prowler near your house. I've kept an eye on it ever since."

"No kidding!" I exclaimed. "I knew that woman had to be good for something."

"Wash your hands," the detective said. "No telling what was on those gloves."

Chapter Twenty-Six

As I waved to Officer Beamer, I turned back to Lenny, who looked tired and a bit frazzled. His normally spunky hair was matted and flat, and his boyish dimple was nowhere to be seen. I searched for a little levity to pacify his nerves.

"That was a close one, huh? I thought Beamer was going to cuff us and stuff us for sure."

"I don't know if giving him the gloves was a good idea, Em," he said, unlocking his car door. "I mean, for all he knows, *we're* the murders."

I nodded. "I know. I thought about that. But what else could I do? I had to give him something. I had to tell him why we were there."

"True," Lenny agreed. "And he did seem to buy our story."

"Of course he did. It was the truth!"

His lips turned up at the corners, and a hint of his dimple returned. "After all that's happened, you still believe in truth and justice and happily ever after?"

I put my hands in my pockets. "I suppose you think I'm foolish."

"No, that's the problem. I don't. Why do you think I keep getting tangled up in all this?"

From the motion of his hands, one would have thought 'all this' could have been plucked from the sky.

"I'm sorry," I said.

"I'm not," he said, smirking as he got into the car. "Get some sleep, Em. Austin's memorial service is tomorrow. We'll need our energy if you intend to keep up this game of cat and mouse."

Sleep, I thought as I walked up my front steps. I couldn't count on it. My mind was too filled with timelines and suspects and motives. It had been nine days since Austin's death, and what did we know for certain? We knew the gloves in fact had been hidden—but if not by the murderer, then by whom? It had to have been Alex—Alex or Dan—and my money was on Alex. He must have thought he was protecting his precious theater from liability, but that didn't make sense either. The gloves would have proven that Austin was indeed wearing protective gear. Why would he want to dispose of them?

I switched on the bathroom light and washed my hands thoroughly. Obviously Alex, Dan, or somebody from the theater building had found Austin, removed the gloves, and stashed them under the mattress. There must have been something on or in the gloves, some telltale sign of wrongdoing, that would prompt someone to dispose of them. Or perhaps the gloves themselves were defective or damaged—punctured or ripped. As I washed my face vigorously, I attempted to visualize the gloves but nothing particular came to mind. They appeared like any other pair of industrial gloves. I reached for a towel. If only I hadn't given the gloves to Detective Beamer. If only I'd been able to examine them in the light of day.

I changed into my pink and red pajamas dotted with the word *amour*, a Valentine's present to myself years ago, and slipped into bed. The gloves were gone. There was no use thinking about them anymore. But it was like André and Paris—a prospect that often kept me awake. Think about them I did for the next hour or more, making superficial connections that eventually unraveled the deeper I went. Frustrated, I turned over my pillow, burying my head in the cool freshness of it. There must have been something or someone else I had forgotten about, but what or whom?

When I awoke the next morning, it came to me. Robert Reynolds, Austin's ROTC instructor. He was the only teacher I hadn't spoken with. I had been so caught up in retracing Austin's last day, I had forgotten all about Reynolds. And if I remembered correctly, the article in the school newspaper said Reynolds knew Austin's family. Here was an angle that looked new and promising, especially as I remembered Austin's discontent as he talked about his stepfather. Perhaps a friend of the family such as Robert Reynolds would know the story behind the family circumstances.

I looked at the clock. Seven thirty a.m. Since I didn't have class, I had plenty of time to stop by the Department of Military Science before Austin's memorial service. I just needed a cup of coffee, a shower, another cup of coffee, and a to-go mug—in that order.

THE MORNING AIR cooled my warm face as I stepped out on my front porch. Although I rarely wore suits, I'd donned a black one today for the memorial service. I wore no coat over the suit jacket, just a brilliant blue scarf and matching blue-black earrings. The suit pants were slightly flared at the bottom to reveal my low-slung heals.

I walked quickly down Oxford Street. As I approached campus and the trees cleared, I noted the dull-gray sky and wondered if it might rain. The air was suspiciously calm, and I scolded myself for forgetting an umbrella on the one day I wanted my hair to look presentable. *Oh well*, I thought as I checked the nape of my neck. My twist was still securely in place. As long as the wind didn't pick up, I still had a chance of looking acceptable for the memorial.

Military Science was located in a small building on campus called Hull House. This I had found out with a quick search of our university's website before I left. I knew the building; it was close to our commons and looked like a little brick house. The inside, though, had been thoroughly gutted and didn't resemble a home in any way. The stairs were metal and led to a metallic catwalk off of which were several rooms.

I scanned a sign posted near the front entrance. Robert Reynolds was located in office number four.

As I walked past doors, searching for number four, I was surprised how different this atmosphere was from the rest of the campus. It seemed more official, more businesslike. Several men were dressed in Army uniforms and walked quickly and with purpose. "Ma'am," they repeated briefly as my eyes met theirs. I concentrated hard on not blushing, but the task proved difficult. By the time I found room number four, I decided I liked the pressed clothes, shiny boots, and sense of urgency. Reynolds confirmed this decision when he quickly stood up from his desk and said, "Yes, ma'am? May I help you?" when I entered the room.

I silently celebrated my luck at finding him in his office.

Reynolds was an older gentleman, close to seventy, and sported a pair of square-lensed glasses and a graying crew cut. He wasn't in uniform but wore a red short-sleeved polo that showed off his well-defined arms.

I stuck out my hand, and he shook it firmly, all business. I knew I could cut no corners of my explanation with this man. "I'm Emmeline Prather, and I teach in the English Department. I would like to talk to you about Austin Oliver. We both had him in our classes."

"Of course, Ms. Prather. Please, take a seat."

I sat down, and he sat back down behind his desk. I noted how orderly it was and free of clutter. I was pretty sure that with an identical three-tiered bin I could accomplish something similar.

"Austin's memorial is today," I began, perching lightly on the edge of the cushion.

"Yes, ma'am. I'm aware of that."

"I plan on going, of course."

He didn't acknowledge my response; instead he took off his glasses and cleaned them.

"I suppose you'll attend as well. I read in the paper that you knew his family," I said, straightening my shoulders.

He put his glasses back on. "Yes, ma'am. I once knew his mother. She lives on a farm about two hundred miles north of here with her husband."

I nodded. "I suppose you knew Austin quite well then, too."

"No, ma'am, I didn't."

I remained silent. I was no stranger to the unspoken rules of hardball.

"I knew Austin's grandfather. He and I both grew up on farms near Milbank and were only too happy to join the Army when we turned eighteen. Not many other ways for poor kids like us to see the world. I only knew Austin's mom, Patricia, when she attended school here for a time."

I furrowed my brows. "Here at Copper Bluff?"

He nodded. "Yes, ma'am. That's correct."

My austere façade was beginning to crumble with each new piece of information he revealed. I tried, unsuccessfully, to remain reserved. "Well … what … huh."

I'm certain he estimated my response—or at least my speaking capabilities—to be below average. He continued more sympathetically. "Her father had big plans for her education. Told me so when he brought her here. He was a general in the Army. I don't know if I said that."

An idea was forming in my mind. "What did she get her degree in?"

"Unfortunately, she could not complete her course work," he said.

"Why not?"

"Ma'am?" he questioned.

For a moment, I wondered if I had spoken the previous words aloud. "Why couldn't she complete her coursework?"

Now his aspect changed, and I thought I saw his cheeks redden. Had I embarrassed him?

"She was with child, ma'am. She got herself into trouble with some fraternity boy."

She got *herself* into trouble? That would be an interesting feat indeed. I wanted to say something, but I knew there was no way of correcting him and still continuing our conversation. "Of course. She was pregnant with Austin. I suppose you don't know who the father was?"

Now his look turned to one of irritation. He scowled at me as if I were a girl fresh out of high school. "Of course not. We never used to speak of such things."

I took my scolding good-naturedly and attempted to look ashamed. Secretly, though, I was brimming with theories. "No, certainly not. I apologize." I waited a long moment before continuing. "So ... I assume Patricia Oliver never returned to campus?"

He folded his hands in front of him on the desk. "No. As an unwed mother, she was forced to move back to the family farm up near Milbank. That's how she met her new fella, I suppose. The Olivers were neighbors of theirs." Now Reynolds released a thoughtful sigh. "It's funny how things come full circle, isn't it, Ms. Prather? The general never wanted anything to do with the farm—got rid of it the day Patricia married. But who did she turn around and marry? A farmer." He shook his head.

"Ironic, isn't it?" I said.

"I suppose that's the word you young folks would use. I prefer the word shame. A crying shame."

"It is that too," I said, standing up from my chair. "Except the

Olivers are selling their farmland as well. Perhaps the general would have found some consolation in that."

He stood also.

"Thank you so much for your time," I said, shaking his hand with enthusiasm. Old-fashioned or not, he had given me the information I needed to solve Austin's murder. For that I would be forever grateful.

"The pleasure is mine," he said politely.

I pushed open the door of Hull House and noticed the gray morning had turned darker, charcoal almost, and the October wind had picked up as well. I quickened my step toward the library.

Reynolds had said that Patricia Oliver was involved with a fraternity man on campus, and it hadn't taken long for me to determine which fraternity. That's why Austin had been so desperate to join—not because of his own interests, but because his biological father had been a member. I thought back to the long row of framed pictures in the study of the fraternity, and my theory made perfect sense. All I needed was confirmation, and I knew just where to look.

The Hoover Library was my favorite place on campus. It wasn't old, and it wasn't named for President Herbert Hoover but a retired history professor of the same name. It was built in the 1970s and had a lot of square windows filled with ordinary houseplants. Although at first I found this odd, it was probably why I ended up liking the place so much. The eclectic assortment of plants gave the library the touch it needed to make it seem familiar and homey.

I walked through the security scanner and directly up two flights of stairs. The third floor emanated a strong smell of old books that was noticeable the moment one stepped onto the floor. The books seemed so much more important than the new books on the first floor because, in some respects, they were. Many of the sections housed books, periodicals, and newspapers that had never seen the light of a digital scanner. They were originals.

As I progressed farther, the plants were replaced by dust. Walking by some of the windows created a stir of particles that wafted halfway up the window before they slowly fell back down again. I began scanning aisles, looking for the university's yearbooks, which had still been popular and in print eighteen years ago. It took me several minutes to find the bookshelf and much longer to find the year I was searching for. My mouth went dry as I pulled the yearbook off the shelf.

Crouching down, I flipped through it rather shakily, examining each page carefully but quickly. Even eighteen short years made the students seem somewhat antiquated when compared to today. Back then men still wore suits and ties, and women, dresses or blouses.

I turned one page, then another, then another, then stopped. I put the book on the floor, smoothing the crease down the middle. Looking back at me was a young man with small crinkled eyes and a familiar grin. A fraternity man. I knew in an instant it was Austin's biological father.

Chapter Twenty-Seven

IT HAD TAKEN only ten days for the university to organize a memorial for Austin. It would take place in Pender Auditorium over the lunch hour, from twelve to twelve fifty. Since no classes were held from twelve to one in the afternoon, this meant anyone who wanted to be there could attend. Pender was one of the larger—and more beautiful—auditoriums on campus. It had a charming ceiling with a depiction of the birth of Venus more modest than Botticelli's painting. Venus stood in a seashell with her lovely long hair concealing her body's private places, the blue ocean and sky surrounding her.

I headed for my office. I desperately wanted to tell Lenny what I had found out before the memorial service, but there simply wasn't enough time to find him in between his Tuesday classes.

Giles's door was open, so I knew he was in, but I quickly slipped into my office and shut the door before anybody had a chance to intrude. I needed a moment before the memorial service to gather my thoughts—and reapply my lipstick.

I stood at my window and looked out. On campus, nothing had changed but the weather; the mild days of September had turned into the bitter nights of October. Students gushed out of one building and into another, full of vitality and confidence in the future. One student was absent, though—*my* student— and now the story that had eluded me before seemed almost complete. The fragments of Austin Oliver's life were forming a narrative I would be entrusted to tell, and tell it I would when the time was right and my suspicions confirmed.

Revitalized by my new sense of purpose and a squirt of body spray, I peeked into Giles's office to remind him about the memorial.

"Look at this, Emmeline! Everything on my screen has been … miniaturized."

I smiled as I came up behind him. Though my computer was old, I could still get Giles out of most of his computer jams. I relied heavily on programs for my daily work. "I see the problem. See here? You're only at fifty percent screen size." I clicked the down arrow in Microsoft Word and selected two hundred percent. "There."

"I cannot imagine how that came to be. I've never touched that menu in my life," said Giles.

I walked back toward the door, hiding my smile. The truth was I had caught him several times changing his font, background, and even screen resolution—the screen resolution being the worst of his problems. For two days he hadn't used his computer at all.

"I suppose you're on your way to the memorial," said Giles, saving his work.

"Yes. Are you going?"

"In a minute. If you want to wait, I'll walk with you." He shrugged into his corduroy jacket.

"That's okay. I promised Ann Jorgenson I'd stop by. I'm heading that way now."

"Well then, I'll see you there," said Giles.

I walked halfway down the hallway, approaching the

suspended passageway. Then I stopped and turned around. Straight down the hall was my office and Giles's. Giles was shutting his door.

"Did you forget something?" Giles asked.

"No, it's nothing," I said and kept walking. But actually I had remembered something very, very important.

Ann was in her office but didn't notice me as I approached, so I knocked lightly. "Ann?"

"Em! Come in. I'm just printing out my advisee list. It grows every semester. I seem to be the catchall for other departments."

"I feel for you." Still standing at the door, I looked down the hall to make sure no one could overhear. "Hopefully that will change soon?" I asked quietly.

She nodded her head slightly. "It looks encouraging."

"That's great news. It will be so much better for you. How does Owen feel about it?"

She rolled her eyes. "You know men. They hate change, but they're totally persuadable."

I laughed. "I'm on my way to the memorial. Do you want to walk together?"

She stood up. "That's right! I'm supposed to meet Owen. I'm so glad you reminded me. Just let me grab my jacket." She pulled on a North Face jacket that made her seem more like a student than a professor, and I was surprised by her lack of attention to her attire. She didn't appear appropriately dressed for a memorial service. She must have forgotten.

We walked down the stairs toward Pender Hall in a slight drizzle that made the sidewalk slick. Out of earshot of her department chair, she spoke more freely of Owen's new position. It sounded more like a probability than a possibility.

"Have you talked to their Women's Studies Department?" I asked, pulling my suit jacket tighter. The wind really did make any kind of activity that much more strenuous.

"That's the beauty of it," said Ann. "I *know* the chair—

Chelsea James. We went to school together at Columbia. She's the one who got Owen his interview."

"Nice," I said. "It makes getting in that much easier."

"Tell me about it," she said, waving to one of her students.

We turned toward the mountain of steps leading up to the auditorium. They were slippery from the drizzle, and I held onto the handrail as we ascended. "I suppose you'll miss climbing these stairs, for I'm certain they know what the Americans with Disabilities Act is. Perhaps they even make accommodations for it."

Ann laughed. "I'm sorry to say I won't miss it. I'm so tired of this small town; I can't wait to get to the Cities."

"I bet Owen will, though. Didn't he go to college here?"

"God, yes. He loves it—his alma mater. But it will do him good to experience another campus. Otherwise, he'll just get inbred. You know what I mean?"

I nodded, even though I didn't. I empathized completely with Owen. I would stay here the rest of my days if God and the dean willed it. When people said change was good, all they meant was that change was good for them. And the change would certainly benefit Ann.

I wiped my heels on the mat of the landing as students moved past us in droves. I was surprised to see so many students here, and I wondered if they'd all known Austin personally. Ann held the door for me as we entered the auditorium, motioning toward the area reserved for faculty and staff.

"I guess we sit there. I don't see Owen ... do you?"

I scanned the rows of faculty members, but it was impossible to tell from this far away. I shook my head.

"I'm just going to wait here," said Ann. "I'll meet you down there in a few."

"Okay," I said and headed toward the first six rows of seats. I spotted Lenny in the second row. He was wearing a classic brown-checked blazer and royal blue tie, and if I didn't know better, I would have said the tie was for me.

"Hey," he said as I scooted in next to him. "I saved you a seat."

"Thanks," I said, meeting his eyes. "Not just for the seat, but for everything. I don't know what I would have done last night without you."

His eyes held mine a moment longer before he replied, "Of course, Em. I'd do anything for you."

I inhaled sharply, the breath sticking deep in my lungs.

He leaned in confidentially. "This tie? It's just the tip of the iceberg," he said, flipping it over.

A smile spread across my face and his too. Then he sat back in his chair.

I looked around the auditorium to see who was in attendance. "Look who showed up after his late night." I nodded in Alex's direction. He was seated across the aisle in the first row.

"I think everyone's expected to participate," said Lenny.

"He certainly didn't come of his own volition," I said. "Look at poor Dan. He looks perfectly miserable sitting next to Alex." Dan's shoulders rounded just enough to make him look small and weak next to Alex, whose black sports jacket was at least a size forty-eight.

Most of the rows on the floor were filled, and fewer and fewer students were trickling in to the balcony. President Conner, a sagging man in his late sixties, came up to the podium, checked the microphone, and walked back toward the folding chairs on stage.

"He's getting ready to begin," I said, glancing toward the back door. "Where's Ann?" She stood in the same place I left her, presumably waiting for Owen. He should have been here by now.

"There's Owen," said Lenny, motioning toward the corner of the stage, near the curtain.

"What's he doing up there?"

Unlike Ann, Owen had not forgotten about the memorial. He was dressed in black from head to toe. "He's talking to

Austin's mother," I said. Austin's stepfather was seated next to her.

Lenny looked baffled, but I didn't have time to explain. "I'd better go get Ann." As I stood up, though, I realized Ann had spotted Owen, too, for she was hastily moving toward the front of the auditorium.

Ann waved at Owen, trying to gain his attention. When she did, she motioned for him to sit down, and he walked off the stage, looking slightly dazed by all the people in the hall.

She sat in an end seat, two rows behind us. "Can you move down, Claudia? I don't think Owen has a seat."

Claudia looked around. "Of course," she said, but there was obviously nowhere for her to move. There were no more seats in that row. She stood and found a seat several rows behind us, right next to Giles.

Making his apologies as he approached, Owen sat down slowly next to Ann.

"Is something wrong?" I heard Ann whisper. "Who is that?"

"No ... I .... It's someone I used to—"

Just then, President Conner began to speak, and I turned my attention to the stage. "Welcome students, faculty, and friends of Austin Oliver, a young man who had just begun his studies but had already proven himself an important part of our university. I want to extend a special welcome to the Olivers, Craig and Patricia, who had much to be proud of in their son Austin."

Now it became obvious to everyone that these were his parents. His mother had the same wide cheekbones and tanned, kind face. She had the same youthful look of the outdoors about her. She was dressed in a long black skirt and blouse, and a sand-colored braid hung down the middle of her back. Austin's father looked nothing like him. He was a small man with dark, thinning hair. One could tell because his head was inclined; his eyes, perhaps to hide his tears, never left the floor.

Patricia approached the podium at the president's cue. "I agreed to speak for a few moments," she began, "because I knew how important the university had become to Austin. It was a fresh start, a new beginning."

When she spoke, I noticed she had the same tentative speech patterns as Austin. She wasn't used to addressing a large group of people, yet she wasn't exactly uncomfortable in front of a crowd. Her circle was smaller, as was Austin's. That was all.

Patricia smiled briefly, but tears were beginning to form in her eyes. "It takes an enormous amount of courage to do something different, to be something different. Austin had that courage …." She faltered then began again. "We are trying to have courage, too, to face these days without him. I hope we can count on you for your support."

Applause thundered through the auditorium as row after row began to stand to show their support of this woman and their classmate, and I couldn't have been prouder of our university than at that moment. I stood in solidarity with my colleagues, applauding her courage and wherewithal.

President Conner motioned for everyone to be seated so that the memorial could continue, but I couldn't focus on any of the other speakers. All I could think about was a way to speak to Mrs. Oliver in private after the program. I knew there would be coffee and cookies, but perhaps I could pull her aside before the reception. After all, there was still a murderer at large on the campus.

I refocused my attention on the speakers as I saw Sarah approach the podium, a small sheet of white paper in her hand.

Lenny jabbed me hard in the side.

"I know," I said. "I see her."

All became clear within seconds, however, as I realized she was reading the eulogies composed by her creative writing class. She couldn't have looked more beautiful in her black sweater dress and knee-high boots—or sounded more the part. Her voice had a quality meant for the stage; she was the consummate actress. When she was finished, she handed the paper to Austin's mother as a memento from the student body, ending the memorial service with the perfect touch. President Conner said a few brief concluding words and directed everyone to the lobby for refreshments and fellowship, and the people on the stage, including the Olivers, vanished behind the side curtain.

"Blast it! I hoped to talk to her," I whispered to Lenny. Students and faculty were out of their seats, in the aisles, and at the door. It was sudden chaos.

"It looks like you're just going to have to wait. We're not moving anytime soon," said Lenny.

I stood up. "I'm going to see if I can find her. Wait for me at the reception."

Lenny shook his head. "You're never going to get through."

I shimmed past coworker after coworker with "excuse me, pardon me, sorry" dropping from my lips. For Jane Lemort I saved an especially humble "I'm so very sorry" when I accidentally stepped on her foot, exposed by open-toed heels.

"Well I never!" was her response.

When I made it to the aisle, I walked quickly up the stairs, left of the stage, but all was quiet behind the curtain. I walked a bit farther, all the way to the back door, and peered out, but no one was there.

I turned back toward the stage and the crush of the auditorium; thankfully, it had cleared some. There were still several people mulling about by the doors, waiting for a break in the crowd. When none appeared, I made my way through with a few hectic motions. It was surprising how quickly people acquiesced when they thought there was some sort of emergency.

The smile on my face was short-lived as it met with the very stern brow of Detective Beamer. Immediately I affected an air of nonchalance, shuffling toward the reception area like a fifteen-year-old.

"Ms. Prather. What seems to be the emergency?"

"Huh?" I managed a yawn. "No emergency. Nothing at all."

He crossed his arms, looking very much like a cop. "It didn't look like nothing when you mowed down those kids."

"Who, them?" I laughed. Now I was standing close enough to ask him a question. I leaned in conspiratorially. "Did you find out anything, about the gloves, I mean?"

He looked so serious in his wool jacket and hat that I wondered if my question would warrant an answer at all. Then he surprised me by quirking an eyebrow and whispering, "Did *you* find out anything about the gloves last night?"

Now it was my turn to be serious. I took a step back. "Well, no, I didn't. You didn't really give me a chance."

"You were in the theater with the gloves for quite some time. I thought maybe you *smelled* something on them." Now both of his eyebrows were arched and encouraging.

"Smelled?" I thought back to my time under the bed with the gloves placed on my chest. They didn't smell bad; I would remember. Yet there was something about them, some particular smell. I squeezed my eyes shut, helping my memory along. It was almost pleasant …. My eyes flew open. "Ether! They smelled like ether!"

I clasped my hand over my mouth. Now Officer Beamer would know Sophie had told me about the ethylene chlorohydrin.

"Don't worry, Professor. I had a feeling you knew more about Austin's death than you let on last night, so I asked Sophie this morning if she had talked to you about the case. She admitted she had. And before you start making excuses for her," he said, holding up his hand like a stop sign, "let me tell you that she wasn't reprimanded."

He smiled, and I knew Sophie would be fine.

"Does this mean … I know what it means." I grabbed his shoulder, and he lowered his head to mine. "It means the gloves *were* the murder weapon."

He touched the rim of his wool hat. "You have yourself a good day, Ms. Prather. I have a reception to secure."

I stood open-mouthed, watching Beamer walk away. He had as much as told me what I wanted to know. That's why the murderer was so desperate to get the gloves back. They weren't just evidence; they were the weapon used to kill Austin.

I walked trance-like toward the reception, pulling each string together like a puppeteer preparing for the final act. It all began to make sense, all of it. My pulse quickened. If my deductions were all true, someone else was in danger, someone to whom I owed it to save.

I broke into a run, dodging students and faculty members alike. This time, I didn't bother with apologies. I ran headlong down the hallway toward the main lobby. I quickly scanned the area and each freshly pressed white linen-clad table. President Conner and Mr. Oliver were near the front, several students were gathering at the dessert table, but Mrs. Oliver was nowhere to be found. I hesitated. Should I stay and keep looking, or should I go look elsewhere?

I saw Lenny getting a cup of coffee and yelled in his direction. This was no time for manners. "Lenny!"

Several others turned around as well as Lenny.

He hurried over. "Jesus! What is it?"

"Mrs. Oliver. Is she here?"

He shook his head. "No. I heard Conner say she stepped outside to get some air."

"Let me know if you see her," I said. "I think she's in grave danger."

I didn't bother waiting for Lenny's inevitable retort; I dashed out the door and toward the auditorium. I stopped, looking down each direction of the hallway. I heard voices—but where? Outside! They were coming through the double doors of the landing. I flung open the doors to reveal the stunned face of one of my students.

"Adam? What are you doing here?" The words tumbled out of my mouth before I could catch them.

"Professor Prather?" Adam said.

"Never mind. Have you seen a lady with blonde hair, a braid about down to here, and a long black skirt?"

He looked down the stairs and back at me.

"Well?" I said, stomping my foot.

"Professor, I think the woman you're describing just fell down the stairs."

I rushed onward and found Mrs. Oliver on the second landing, surrounded by at least a dozen students. Racing down the stairs, I nearly tripped on the slick, worn concrete. I grabbed the handrail just in time. "Is she breathing?" I called down. Several students nodded in my direction.

"Adam!" I called. "Go to the main lobby. Get Officer Beamer. Tell him Mrs. Oliver has been hurt!"

The students made way for me as I approached Mrs. Oliver. I bent down on one knee, checking for a pulse and found it. I looked around at their faces. "Who did this? Did you see anyone flee? In what direction?"

They all stared back at me blankly. A few shook their heads. A boy with glasses finally said, "I think she just tripped."

Mrs. Oliver's eyes began to flutter. Then she moved her hands as if trying to sit up. Her efforts failed dismally, and she stopped. Instead her lips parted, and she said, "*I was pushed.*"

I stood up, surveying the campus from the landing. A few students were scattered here and there; otherwise, there was limited activity. The rain was coming down more steadily now. I bent down and shielded Mrs. Oliver's face with my suit jacket.

I heard the sudden push of the double doors and knew it was Beamer. "Down here!" I yelled.

"Is she alive?" he said, as he took the stairs two at a time.

"Yes. She says she was pushed. And I know who pushed her."

Chapter Twenty-Eight

BEAMER RADIOED TO Sophie, asking her to secure the perimeter, then motioned for another officer to stay with Mrs. Oliver until the ambulance came. We returned to the lobby, discussing the upcoming scenario. He was willing to go along with it if it would flush out the murderer; I assured him it would, and he was inclined to agree.

The lobby was relatively quiet, with students and faculty talking in hushed tones and sipping coffee or munching cookies. Thus when we entered with a loud clang of the double doors and rosy cheeks, all eyes were on us. All that was required to get their attention was to open my mouth.

"Officer Beamer and I have just come from the site of another unfortunate accident," I proclaimed. With this announcement, several people glanced around as if for reassurance. I saw Giles put his hand to his forehead.

"It's true," said Detective Beamer. "Mrs. Oliver has fallen down the steps outside." Several people gasped audibly, and some of the students began whispering. President Conner, who was standing next to Mr. Oliver, gestured for Mr. Oliver to sit down.

"It will come as no shock to *one* of you when I say Patricia Oliver's accident just now was no accident at all. Like her son, Mrs. Oliver has had an attempt on her life made right here on this same campus—and by the same person."

"What?" could be heard trickling through the whispers.

"Professor Prather, are you certain you know what you're saying?" asked Dean Richardson.

Lenny wasn't far from Dean Richardson. The look on his face told me to make sure I did before I opened my mouth in front of the entire faculty.

I nodded vigorously in Lenny's direction. "Quite certain, Dean Richardson. If you let me continue, I'll explain." Since he didn't raise any other objections, I proceeded. "It is not surprising, really. There are several reasons why one person would want to kill another: hatred, jealousy, fear, self-preservation. The human condition endures on strong emotions. Several people had reason enough to kill Austin, but only one of you did."

I looked out at the sea of faces, all of them familiar and unsuspecting. It was hard to believe I was standing in the same room as the killer.

Sarah Sorenson was sitting next to her boyfriend, Sean, at the table directly in front of me. She was watching me with keen interest and was visibly surprised when I said her name out loud. "Sarah, by your own admission, you were the last person to see Austin alive."

"Yes?" Sarah said questioningly.

"Perhaps you were angry at Austin for partying with the fraternity. Maybe you had heard about his leaving the party with a mystery girl, a girl he seemed to be spending more and more time with."

"Professor Prather, you know that's not true!" she said, shocked by my line of reasoning. "I wasn't his girlfriend! I'm Sean's girlfriend." She pointed to Sean, who sat rigid beside her. "Tell them, Sean!"

Sean frowned, probably angry with her for pulling him into her predicament.

"Yes, tell us, Sean, how jealous you had become of Austin for taking your girlfriend on all sorts of excursions—poetry readings, for instance. Not something likely to interest a chemistry major."

"I knew they were just friends. She wasn't into him." He crossed his arms.

"Being a chemistry major, you probably knew a little something about the poison that killed him. "

A couple of girls standing behind him backed away.

"I have no idea what you're talking about," said Sean. "I'm just a sophomore. I've hardly had any chemistry yet."

My eyes moved to the next table. "But sophomores aren't that stupid, are they, Jared?" Jared, looking dapper in his black Polo shirt, attempted to hide behind another student, but he was too tall. I walked several steps in his direction. "You knew that Austin was smart, and what's more, he was charismatic. Students were charmed by his easy ways. And that bothered you, didn't it? It bothered you that a nobody from a farm challenged your popularity in the fraternity."

"Nah. It wasn't like that," said Jared, shifting in his seat. "I was just giving him a hard time."

"And did giving him a hard time include murdering him?" I asked.

"No way! Do you think I'm stupid?"

I didn't answer that question; instead I moved toward the faculty, gathered on the left side of the room. Most of them had been leaning forward but now leaned back as I approached. "We're not stupid, are we? We're pretty smart—we have our PhDs, our MBAs, our MFAs. But is one of us smart enough to pull off a murder?" I paused and shook my head. "It appears not."

"I don't appreciate having accusations thrown at us as if we were common street criminals!" boomed Alex.

I smiled. "I bet you don't, considering the murder took place in your department. How exactly did Austin come in contact with ethylene chlorohydrin? Tell us, Alex, how do you use it in the theater?"

Alex drew his palms together, tapping his index fingers. "Look, you're right. We sometimes use it in the theater to make dye, but Photography also uses it as a solvent. Either way, Austin could not have come into contact with it. He was a volunteer, for christ's sake!"

I nodded. My guess had paid off. I knew he had access to either the chemical or something similar. "But you couldn't be sure. That's why you hid the gloves Austin wore under Fantine's bed. You recognized the ether smell when you discovered the body. You knew how bad it looked for the theater, so rather than calling the police, you simply left Austin for the janitor to discover."

"Is that true?" asked Dan, leaning across the table. Martha Church, who also sat at his table, was waiting patiently for his answer.

Alex looked around the room. All eyes were on him, including Beamer's.

"It *is* true—but just wait a minute! Wait a minute!" he continued through the sudden increase in noise. "She didn't say I *killed* him. She said I *found* him. As in, *found him already dead.*"

"That's right," I agreed. "Alex might have done a deplorable act by leaving Austin lying there, but he did not commit the crime. No, that was done by someone Austin knew more intimately, someone he had been pressuring for weeks."

I walked in between the tables, searching for one person in particular, hoping she had made it back in time for my plan to work. Finding her, I continued, "There was something that puzzled me from the start, something I could not fit into Austin's last day on campus. I say *on campus* because he was not in *class* that day, but he was in Harriman Hall. In fact, I myself talked to him. He was near my office, and I thought he was coming to talk to me about the poem he had chosen to read for class. When he left, I noticed he was not wearing his backpack and was not, indeed, on his way to class. So why, then, come to Harriman Hall? Then it came to me. He was not in Harriman Hall at all. He was cutting through it on his way to Windsor Hall. He was on his way to see you, Ann, wasn't he?"

It wasn't Ann's face I noticed but Owen's. It registered both shock and grief, and I knew he'd guessed what I was about to say. Ann showed no such forethought.

"*Em!* Are you serious?" She attempted a laugh. "What do I have to do with any of this?"

I shook my head, a bit disappointed at her antics. "You have everything to do with this, Ann. You were the first person Austin met when he came to the university. You were his advisor."

"So?" she glared. "I have lots of students to advise. Jeez, I just told you, I'm the overflow for other departments!"

"You had the unique opportunity to hear Austin's real reason for attending this university, his *mission*, as one student put it. He was here to meet his biological father."

"Just wait a minute now, just wait," she said, her voice fraught.

But I didn't wait. I advanced toward her. "I bet Austin thought it was a real coincidence that your own last name matched the one he was looking for; it must have been the perfect opportunity for him to gather information about his father and how to go about telling him who he was. Little did he know you hadn't been able to conceive a child, despite your and Owen's desire for one, and that you found his intrusion on your lives a threat to your marriage."

"That's a lie!" Ann said.

Owen stared at her openly. "Austin was my son? I mean, did you know he was my son? I figured at the memorial that that could have been the case, but I just couldn't believe what I was hearing. Patricia and I were going to talk afterward …." The rest of the sentence trailed off.

Ann refocused on Owen. "I didn't do anything, Owen. You have to believe me. Emmeline is *crazy*—certifiably *insane* to say these sorts of things."

I continued on, "When you noticed Austin had signed up for your husband's class, you realized you needed a plan and quick. You stalled him in every way you could, telling him perhaps that Owen didn't want children, that you were prepping him to hear the unwelcome news. You became his confidante, his conspirator."

Owen looked pale. "How can you say these things about Ann? She's your friend."

I shrugged. "Because they're true. I overheard her conversation with Austin the night of the English Department's potluck. I just didn't realize it. She in fact is the woman Austin had been spending so much time with—the woman Sarah became suspicious of."

"I knew it! I knew it was a teacher!" interjected Sarah. "You were the one who was with him the night of the frat party. I asked him if he needed a ride, and he said he already had a *faculty escort* back to the dorms. I knew there was something weird about his joke."

I nodded in Sarah's direction. "Owen's trip to Minneapolis gave Ann the perfect opportunity for one last-ditch effort to persuade Austin that she needed more time. But," I turned to Ann, "even your threats couldn't keep Austin quiet. He became involved in everything you were active in: the poetry reading, the theater. He was relentless in his pursuit. Despite your pleas for more time, he made an appointment with Owen. It was then he was to tell Owen the happy news. Desperate now, you knew you had to get out of Copper Bluff. You scheduled the interview for Owen and called your friend in Women's Studies. When your efforts had no effect on Austin Friday night, you called upon another friend of yours, Martha Church, Saturday. Isn't that true, Martha?"

"It is," exclaimed Martha. "We only met for a moment, though. She needed the code to get into the shop to see the costumes for *Les Mis* ...." I could see Martha connecting the dots that formed a snapshot of Austin's murder.

I nodded in Alex's direction. "So you see, your intuition was right. Austin might not have had access to the poison, but Martha certainly did—and thus so did her friend, Ann Jorgenson." I turned back toward Ann. "It was that day you decided to poison Austin, to kill the only son Owen would have ever known."

Now tears began to form in Ann's eyes. "No, no. I didn't mean to kill him. You're wrong." She turned toward Owen, looking much like a young child about to be scolded. "You have to believe me. I only wanted him to get sick so that he couldn't meet with you on Monday. I just needed a little more time ...."

"How? How could you do this?" whispered Owen.

"I didn't know it was toxic; I swear. When I found it in the costume shop, I figured it was pretty common and that it would cause some skin irritation at most, enough to make him miss the meeting he had scheduled with you. It's not like he swallowed it or anything. I just put it in his gloves."

Martha shook her frizzy head vigorously. "It doesn't cause any noticeable irritation; that's why it's so dangerous. He wouldn't have even known it was there."

"She's right," whispered Owen.

"But *you* use it!" Ann pleaded to Martha. "I saw you using it in the studio."

"I might work in the *Art* Department, but that doesn't mean I'm a moron. I work around hundreds of dangerous paints and chemicals—and know how to use them without endangering someone's life!" Anger and disgust filled Martha's eyes.

Hundreds was a stretch, but I didn't argue.

Losing her quarrel with Martha, Ann returned to Owen. "I was going to check on him. *Please believe me.* That's why I went back to the theater. But you were there," she hissed, turning in Sarah's direction, "And Austin seemed just fine. *Tell them.*"

"He wasn't fine," Sarah shot back. "He was sick and dizzy and ... and sick!"

"You might have even killed him yourself," Ann continued desperately. "How do we know it was even the gloves that killed him?"

I immediately interceded. "Ann, you yourself knew it was the gloves that killed Austin. You broke into my house Friday night after I mentioned being a close friend of Austin's in our committee meeting. You thought that I had met with Austin and that I had the gloves. Knowing my schedule, you knew you could retrieve the evidence of what you had done. That's why you went back to the theater in the first place. Not to check on him."

"It wasn't like that," Ann said. The tears that had been forming in her eyes now ran down her cheeks. "None of it. You're twisting it all around."

"You also knew that, given enough time with my fraternity students, I would have realized Austin wanted to join because his biological father had lived in the same house." I turned to Owen. "I saw your picture, Owen, the day I went to the fraternity to see Jared about a paper."

"That's right. I belonged to the fraternity," said Owen, but he never took his small eyes off of Ann.

"See, Ann, it makes sense. That's why you pushed soon-to-be divorced Patricia Oliver down the stairwell just now. You saw Mrs. Oliver and Owen talking, saw their mutual shock. You couldn't risk the college sweethearts rekindling their relationship or Mrs. Oliver revealing to Owen that Austin was the son she had never told him about. Rather than telling him about Austin years ago and ruining his chances of becoming a famous paleontologist—something he said in his yearbook he dreamed about—Patricia broke off the relationship and dropped out of college. You knew if his birth didn't bring them together, his death certainly would have."

"I know nothing about that!" she said. She sounded truly insulted, and one had to admire her acting skills. "I didn't go to school in this … this Podunk little town. I wanted to get out of here from the moment I stepped foot in this place. I stayed here for you, Owen, at the cost of everything I loved. Even my career."

Owen looked truly baffled now. "You tried to kill her *too*?"

She turned her angry eyes on me. "They have no evidence of that."

I looked at the floor. A small puddle of water marked where she sat. "But Ann, after all that's been said, wouldn't you agree your wet shoes are evidence enough?"

Epilogue

———

As Detective Beamer handcuffed Ann and led her out of the room, I approached the table where Lenny sat. Most of the other English faculty members were there, too, and I felt a bit like a contestant on *The Price is Right* as their eyes followed me toward the vacant spot.

"Well, Emmeline, that was quite a *thing* you did there," said Giles, folding his napkin in tiny squares. "I'm still not sure exactly what you did, and when, but I'm pretty sure it was at the detriment of your English students."

"On the contrary, I'm all caught up on grading papers."

"Nonetheless, there's a rumor going around that your English students might not be your first priority anymore. Could it be that your French students are taking precedence?"

"Score one for the little guy in the beret," said Lenny, holding his Styrofoam cup in the air.

"I haven't had a chance to talk to André yet, but it sounds promising," I said, crossing my legs and deciding my new heels were just as versatile as the Home Shopping Network had promised.

"You've been too busy with what seems to be your new off-campus course: Murder 101," said Giles.

I attempted to raise one eyebrow. "I like the sound of that. I bet enrollment would be phenomenal."

"It still just looks like you have an eyelash," smirked Lenny.

"I have a feeling enrollment is about to skyrocket as it is. Who knows?" Giles hypothesized. "Perhaps this will be the beginning of a new trend in academia, the return of the English major?"

"I wouldn't hold my breath," said Lenny. "One look at Em's syllabus and they'll go running back to hallowed halls of computer science."

I shrugged, taking one of Lenny's uneaten cookies. "Oh well. No one ever said college was for the faint of heart."

Julie Prairie Photography

MARY ANGELA IS the author of *An Act of Murder*, the debut novel in the new Professor Prather mystery series. She is a member of Mystery Writers of America and Sisters in Crime and enjoys reading mysteries as much as writing them. Currently, she teaches English for the University of South Dakota and lives in Sioux Falls with her husband and two young daughters.

For more information, go to maryangelabooks.com.

CPSIA information can be obtained at www.ICGtesting.com
Printed in the USA
LVOW08s1719201016

509596LV00004B/656/P